D1261594

"NORMAN, LOOK WHAT I'VE FOUND!"
HONEY BUNCH EXCLAIMED.

Honey Bunch: Her First Trip in a Trailer

HONEY BUNCH:
HER FIRST TRIP IN A TRAILER

BY
HELEN LOUISE THORNDYKE

AUTHOR OF:
HONEY BUNCH: JUST A LITTLE GIRL
HONEY BUNCH: HER FIRST TRIP ON THE GREAT LAKES
HONEY BUNCH: HER FIRST LITTLE CLUB, ETC.

NEW YORK
GROSSET & DUNLAP
PUBLISHERS

Printed in the United States of America

Copyright, 1939, by
GROSSET & DUNLAP, Inc.

———

All Rights Reserved

Honey Bunch: Her First Trip in a Trailer

CONTENTS

HONEY BUNCH:

HER FIRST TRIP IN A TRAILER

CHAPTER I

THE PRINCESS

"OH, HONEY BUNCH!" shouted Norman Clark. "Ask your mother if you may go!"

The little boy ran across the Morton yard, calling excitedly to Honey Bunch, who was sitting on the front porch eating a cookie.

"Go where, Norman?" Honey Bunch asked quickly. She jumped up from the steps and went to meet her playmate.

"Why, to the puppet show," laughed Norman. "Most everyone in Barham will be there."

"I'd like to see a puppy show!" Honey Bunch exclaimed. "Once my daddy took me—"

"Not a *puppy* show," corrected Norman

with a superior air. "Didn't you ever hear about puppets, Honey Bunch?"

"Oh, puppets," said the little blue-eyed girl.

Of course she knew what they were but she thought she would like to hear her playmate explain them to her, so she said:

"Tell me about puppets, Norman."

The little boy couldn't think of an answer for a minute. While he knew all about the tiny toys himself, it was hard for him to describe them to Honey Bunch.

"Puppets are funny little dolls that jump around and do things like real people," he said slowly. "They talk and act out stories."

"How can dolls act and talk like real people, Norman?" Honey Bunch teased, throwing back her head so that her bright golden curls bobbed around.

"Why, 'cause they have strings tied to 'em. Someone stands behind a curtain and jerks 'em around and does the talking for 'em too. Ask your mother if she'll take us, Honey Bunch. Then you'll see just how it's done."

"Mother went downtown to buy some curtains.   But maybe Mrs. Miller will let me go."

Mrs. Miller had served as housekeeper and laundress for the Morton family ever since Honey Bunch could remember.   The kindly woman loved the little girl dearly, but she had to be careful in everything she did or said, because Honey Bunch liked to imitate her. Sometimes it turned out to be very funny.

The children ran as fast as they could to the kitchen where Mrs. Miller was busy baking. She had just taken a cake from the oven, and her plump face was flushed from the heat of the stove.

"Land sakes, how you do bang that door! You'll spoil my cake!" she exclaimed.   "I sup-pose you're both here for fresh cookies!"

"Oh, Mrs. Miller!" cried the little girl eagerly.   "May I go with Norman to the puppet show?"

"Puppet show?"   The woman looked puzzled for a moment.   Then she laughed.   "Oh, yes, your mother was talking about it only this morning."

"Did she say I might go?"

"Seems to me she did mention she wanted you to see it. It's to be a benefit for the Barham Day Nursery. But I guess she won't get home in time."

"When will Mother come back?" Honey Bunch asked anxiously.

"I'm afraid too late for the marionette show," said Mrs. Miller, explaining that was another name for a puppet show.

Honey Bunch began to wonder if she and Norman might go alone, when the kindly woman made a suggestion.

"I suppose I could take you there myself," she said slowly, looking at the kitchen clock. "I know your mother intended that you should go."

"Oh, Mrs. Miller, please take me!" Honey Bunch cried, catching the housekeeper by the hand and dancing around her. "Norman could go with us. And maybe Ida Camp, too!"

Ida lived in the neighborhood and was one of Honey Bunch's best friends. She and Ida always liked to go places together.

"Land sakes, I don't know if I could look after three of you or not," Mrs. Miller declared.

She gazed down thoughtfully at Norman. He meant to be a good little boy, but sometimes he couldn't help getting into mischief.

"Please take me," begged Norman. "I'll not make a speck of trouble."

"Please take us all," coaxed Honey Bunch sweetly.

"Well, I'll telephone your mother, Norman, and Mrs. Camp," the housekeeper promised. "No use in them making the trip in the hot sun when I'll be going anyway."

As she finished tidying up the pretty kitchen she told the children more about the puppet show. It was to be held in the Community Hall. The show would be given by a Mr. and Mrs. Victor Dare, who toured the country in an automobile with a trailer attached to it.

"One of those moving houses!" cried Honey Bunch. "Oh, I wish my Daddy would buy us one!"

The little girl knew about trailers, for once

in a while one would drive past the door.
Only last Saturday one of the funny rolling
houses had parked out in front of her home and
a nice lady in it had smiled at her.

"You couldn't hire me to live in one of those
stuffy boxes," Mrs. Miller declared. "Why, a
body wouldn't have room enough to swing a
cat."

"You wouldn't swing Lady Clare, would
you?" Honey Bunch asked anxiously.

Mrs. Miller laughed, for Lady Clare was
Honey Bunch's adored black cat. Of course
she hadn't meant that she would like to swing
Lady Clare or any other kitten.

"A trailer hasn't much space," explained the
laundress. "That's what I intended to say."

She went to the telephone and called both
Mrs. Camp and Mrs. Clark. Young Norman's mother was very glad to have him go to
the marionette show with Mrs. Miller.

"Is Ida coming too?" asked Honey Bunch.

"Yes, her mother is sending her over here.
And now I must change my dress."

The housekeeper went upstairs, leaving the

children alone.   Norman, who could not sit
still very long at a time, said:

"Let's have a puppet show of our own!
Come on, Honey Bunch."

The little boy remembered seeing Mrs.
Miller put a ball of string in a kitchen drawer.
This he got and also a whisk broom which she
used for cleaning the couch.   It would be just
right for a puppet.

"This will make a dandy Princess," he declared, tying a piece of string to the end of the
whisk broom.

Honey Bunch stood watching Norman.
She didn't think the whisk broom looked very
much like the Princess of her story book.   But
if the figure had on a pretty dress—

Honey Bunch ran to get a fresh dish cloth,
which she wrapped around the whisk broom.
The bright red border of the dish cloth looked
very nice on the Princess's long trailing skirt.

"We need a Prince too," Norman said.

They could not find another whisk broom,
but Honey Bunch noticed Mrs. Miller's large
cooking fork lying on the stove.

"Oh, there is our Prince!" she cried, picking it up.

The children tied a long string to the handle. For a minute Honey Bunch couldn't decide how to dress the Prince. Then she thought of the black and white dust cloths hanging in the cellarway.

"Now we need a stage," Norman stated when the doll was dressed. "Maybe we could get up on the table and dangle the puppets on the floor."

"I'm afraid Mrs. Miller wouldn't like that," Honey Bunch said doubtfully.

Norman didn't pay any attention. He climbed right up on top the kitchen table. When Honey Bunch saw that the little boy's shoes weren't scratching the shiny top, she scrambled up beside him. The two playmates leaned over the edge, making their marionettes dance on the floor.

"We have to act out a story now," Norman said. "You be the Princess, Honey Bunch. I'm the Prince."

The children became deeply interested in

their play acting and finally lay down on the
table. It was kind of crowded for them.
Without noticing that he was doing so, Norman kept stretching out his legs toward the
cabinet where Mrs. Miller had set her cakes
and cookies.

"Land sakes, what are you doing up on that
table?" a voice cried.

The children had not heard Mrs. Miller
come down the stairs. Norman was so startled
at hearing the woman's voice that he dropped
the Prince. Back went his feet, for he was going to slide off the table. But instead they
went right into the freshly-made layer cake!

"Norman Clark!" exclaimed Mrs. Miller.
"Now see what you've done!"

Her words ended in a little cry of dismay.
In trying to scramble from the table Norman
tilted the cabinet. Down crashed the cake, the
cookies, and a pan of chocolate frosting!

"Now you've ruined everything," cried the
housekeeper. "What will Mrs. Morton say!"

"Oh, and now maybe we can't go to the puppet show!" thought Honey Bunch.

CHAPTER II

THE PUPPET SHOW

"NORMAN CLARK!" exclaimed Mrs. Miller as she stooped to pick up the food. "Such a mess! Why must you always get into mischief?"

"I didn't mean to do it," Norman said, hanging his head. "How did I know the cabinet would tilt?"

"Stand perfectly still until I can wipe your shoes, Norman. You're tracking chocolate icing all over my clean floor. Honey Bunch, get down from that table and don't let me catch you there again!"

The housekeeper spoke crossly, for she had spent more than an hour with the baking. To add to the woman's troubles, Lady Clare padded softly into the kitchen just then. The cat sniffed at the chocolate and started licking it up from the floor.

"We were just playing puppets," Honey

Bunch explained timidly. "We didn't mean
to upset anything."

"You won't make us stay home from the
puppet show?" asked Norman.

"No. I guess it really wasn't your fault.
That cabinet always did tilt easily. But after
this, don't climb up on tables."

While Mrs. Miller mopped the floor, Norman and Honey Bunch went to watch for Ida.
Soon they saw her coming down the street,
dressed in a pretty pink frock.

"Hello," she called. "Are you all ready to
go?"

Mrs. Miller came out of the house just then,
so the four started down the street. The three
children raced ahead, while Mrs. Miller
paused for a moment to tell a neighbor about
the queer puppet accident.

Honey Bunch's mother often said that it was
lucky her housekeeper had a sense of humor,
or she never could have worked for the Morton
family. That was because so many unusual
things seemed to happen in their household.

Honey Bunch—her real name was Gertrude

Marion Morton—tried very hard to be a good child but she couldn't help being a very busy little person. She liked to go to different places, and her daddy, who was a lawyer, had taken her almost everywhere—to the zoo, to the circus, and even up in an airplane. She had traveled on a boat too. Once she went searching for a real buried treasure. Only the past winter she and Ida Camp had formed their own little club—a club with "no boys allowed." Of course Norman, who lived in the house back of the Mortons, had managed to get in. He helped the club members search for Stub, Honey Bunch's country cousin, when the little girl went off to join some gypsies.

Now Honey Bunch was on her way to another kind of fun. Mrs. Miller soon caught up with the children. She made them keep close to her as they drew near the Community Hall.

"Just look at all the people!" cried Norman excitedly.

A long line had formed way out into the street.

"Land sakes, I do believe every seat has been taken," Mrs. Miller gasped.

"Then won't we see the puppet show?" Honey Bunch asked anxiously.

"Yes. But we may have to wait until the next performance."

The laundress and her young charges had taken their places at the end of the line, which moved forward very slowly. Mrs. Miller sighed, for she was tired, and then too she had put on a new pair of shoes which pinched her toes.

Mrs. Miller heaved another deep sigh and said, "Children, it will be at least fifteen minutes before we can get inside the Hall."

Norman too grew weary of waiting. After a while the little boy caught sight of a red auto trailer parked behind the Community Hall.

"It must belong to Victor Dare, the puppet show man," he thought. "I'm going to see if it does."

Without saying a word to Mrs. Miller or Honey Bunch, Norman slipped away. In a moment the laundress missed him. The line was moving up faster now. She was afraid he might not return by the time they reached the ticket office.

"Dear me," she fretted, "where has Norman gone?"

"I think he ran behind the building," declared Ida. "Honey Bunch and I will go after him."

"Then you'll both be lost too. No, stay right here with me." To make certain the girls did not disappear, Mrs. Miller took each by a hand.

Honey Bunch and Ida were worried for fear Norman might not return. The line grew shorter and shorter. At last it was time for Mrs. Miller to buy the tickets.

"Dear me, now what shall I do?" she murmured. "We can't go inside the Hall without Norman."

At that instant Honey Bunch caught sight of the little boy coming around the corner of the building.

"Norman Clark!" she called. "Hurry up or you'll miss the show!"

The chubby fellow ran as fast as he could, sliding into line ahead of the two little girls. The laundress told him that he shouldn't have gone off without letting her know.

"I thought I had lots of time," said Norman. "I didn't suppose the line would move up so fast."

Honey Bunch and Ida could tell that the little boy was rather pleased with himself. While Mrs. Miller was buying the tickets he whispered:

"Guess what I saw back of that building?"

"What, Norman?" asked Honey Bunch softly.

"A big red trailer. I went right inside it too!"

"Were you invited?" questioned Ida Camp.

Norman shook his head. "The door was unlocked and the puppet folks were gone."

"Norman, you didn't go right in!" Ida Camp gasped.

"You shouldn't have done it," Honey Bunch added. She asked quickly, "What was it like, Norman?"

"Oh, just like a little room. There was a
sofa and a stove, and curtains at the win-
dows—"

Norman did not have time to tell any more.
Mrs. Miller hurried the children into the
Community Hall.

"Let's sit up close to the front," urged Norman, pushing forward.

They found seats on the third row. Almost
at once the lights were turned low. A blue
velvet curtain rolled back to reveal a small
stage. The show began.

For a long while the children sat spellbound.
In the play there was a lovely Princess who fell
in love with a handsome Prince, but a mean
witch carried the Princess away to her secret
hut.

Honey Bunch was afraid the Prince might
never find her again. Tears streamed down
the little girl's cheeks. Yet she laughed with
delight when the King's soldiers captured the
witch, returning the Princess to her lover.

The second act made all the children scream
with pleasure. It was about a modern family

which toured the country in their funny auto
trailer. The little dolls moved in such a life-
like way that it was hard for Honey Bunch to
believe they weren't alive. She was curious
to learn how they were pulled about by strings.

The little girl decided she would try to find
out more about it. In the darkened room Mrs.
Miller did not see her slip from her chair and
wander down the aisle. As for Norman and
Ida, their eyes never left the stage. The other
children did not notice Honey Bunch either as
she moved around behind the velvet drop curtain.

Back of the puppet stage a man and a
woman were working very hard making the
dolls act and talk. The little girl saw that the
couple had strings tied to their fingers which
they moved up and down almost as if they were
playing a piano. Honey Bunch kept as still
as a mouse, watching everything the man and
woman did. After a while the couple turned
away from the stage.

"Well, the show's over for another day,"
said the man. "I hope the kiddies enjoyed it."

Just then he noticed Honey Bunch standing close by.

"Hello!" he exclaimed. "Who is our young visitor?"

"I'm Honey Bunch Morton," said the little girl politely. "Are you the Prince's father?"

"Well, not exactly," laughed the man, whose name was Victor Dare. "Unless you might say that all these puppets are my children."

" 'Like the old woman who lived in the shoe, we have so many children we don't know what to do,' " added Mrs. Dare. "Did you like the show?"

"Oh, yes," declared Honey Bunch, " 'specially the Princess. She had such a pretty voice."

Mrs. Dare was glad to hear this because she had spoken the lines for the Princess. When she was a little girl she had always wished she were a lovely Princess.

"What will you do with all your dolls now that the show is over?" inquired Honey Bunch.

"We'll put them to bed in their suitcases,"

replied Mr. Dare. "Each one has its own little bed suitcase. Then we'll carry them to the next town in our trailer."

The little girl asked a great many other questions. Mr. Dare and his wife didn't seem to mind. Nor did they tell her to run away as some grown-ups might have done. They explained how they traveled from town to town in their red trailer, giving puppet shows in many auditoriums.

"Is that your big red trailer back of the building?" asked Honey Bunch. "Norman was—" She stopped just in time because of course she didn't wish to tell tales.

"We make our home in it," said Mrs. Dare, "and see the country at the same time. It's nice not to have to go home when you're away. You just pull your house along and there it is when you want it!"

Honey Bunch laughed. "Oo-ee, that must be fun! I wish I could look inside your trailer some time."

"You shall right away," promised Mrs. Dare.

"I'm carrying out a box of puppets now," added her husband. "Come along if you like, little girl."

Honey Bunch followed the man through the rear door to a parking lot by the alley. As she hurried along she became very excited. What fun this was! But she never once thought that Mrs. Miller might be searching for her.

The laundress really was very worried about Honey Bunch. When the theatre lights went on, she noticed the vacant chair by the aisle. She could not imagine what had become of the little Morton girl.

"Ida, did you see her go away?" she asked.

Honey Bunch's playmate shook her head.

"Why no," she replied. "I guess I was too int'rested in the show to notice."

Norman did not know what had become of Honey Bunch either.

"Maybe she went to the drinking fountain," he suggested. But the little girl was not there.

"I'll look up on the stage and back of the curtain," the little boy offered.

By this time Honey Bunch was in the trailer,

so of course Norman did not find her.   He
came back to report this to Mrs. Miller.

"She can't be far away," declared the
woman.   "I saw her only a few minutes ago.
Perhaps she went to sit with one of her little
friends."

The laundress walked through the Hall.
She asked several of the children who were
still there if they had seen Honey Bunch.   No
one had.

"I think a nice lady with a big blue car
drove Honey Bunch home," said one little girl
to Ida Camp.

"Yes, Mrs. Graham did take a carload of
children a few minutes ago," said Mrs. Miller
when Ida reported what she had heard.

"Probably Honey Bunch went with her,"
said Norman.   "Let's go home."

The laundress did not worry any more over
the little girl.   She felt certain she would find
her at home.   With Ida and Norman she
started for the Morton place, never dreaming
that Honey Bunch had been left behind, and
with strangers, too!

CHAPTER III

AN ANNOYING DOG

MRS. MILLER could not find Honey Bunch anywhere when she reached the Morton home. Mrs. Clark had not seen the little girl drive up in a car nor had any of the neighbors. By that time the laundress was very upset for she was afraid the little girl had been lost.

"I can't imagine what became of the child," she said anxiously. "Her mother will be frantic when she gets home."

"Don't you worry, Mrs. Miller," Norman told her. "Ida and I will help you hunt."

Of course Honey Bunch did not know that she was causing anyone worry. She was having such a nice time assisting Mr. Dare to carry his things to the shiny red trailer.

"Now up you go!" laughed the man as he lifted her through the door.

Honey Bunch caught her breath in delight.

Why, the trailer was even nicer than a play-house! There was a little table which folded right up against the wall, a tiny stove, a re-frigerator, and even a tiled shower bath. On the couch, curled up in a round ball, lay a yellow cat.

"Is that your kitty?" asked the little girl.

"Yes, that's Tommy," replied Mr. Dare. "He's been all over the country with us."

"I have a kitty too," said Honey Bunch. "Lady Clare has been broadened a lot."

"Broadened?" inquired the man.

"Mrs. Miller says that travel is very broad-ening," explained Honey Bunch. "Lady Clare has been almost everywhere just like Tommy."

"Oh, I see," laughed the puppet show man.

"Lady Clare has never been anywhere in a trailer," Honey Bunch went on. "I wish my Daddy would buy one."

The little girl went over to the couch and stroked Tommy's soft fur. He was a very nice cat, but not as nice as Lady Clare, of course.

"Do you want to stay here a minute?" asked Mr. Dare. "I'm going back into the building for another load of scenery. There's Tommy's collar. You might put it on him."

"I'll play with Tommy," said Honey Bunch contentedly.

The cat seemed to like the little girl for he began to purr and rub against her hand. She picked up the cat's beautiful brown leather collar with a row of stones on it.

"You're a very lucky kitty cat to have such a nice collar," she said as she started to put it around Tommy's neck.

Just then the animal gave a little fitt-fitt sound like cats do when they become startled or angry. Honey Bunch looked up quickly to see what had frightened Tommy. She saw that a large stray dog had come up to the door of the trailer.

"Gr-r-r!"

"Don't be afraid, Tommy," she told the cat. "That dog won't bother you here."

But Tommy had his own idea about the matter. He leaped right off the couch onto a tall pile of painted scenery which Mr. Dare hadn't had time to put away. At the same moment Honey Bunch sprang up to close the door of the trailer.

She was too late!

The bold dog pushed his way in. He began barking loudly at the pet cat.

"Go away, you bad dog!" cried Honey Bunch.

The animal paid no attention to her. When the little girl tried to catch hold of him he turned and snapped at her.

"Mr. Dare! Mr. Dare!" called Honey Bunch.

She did not blame Tommy for being afraid of the ugly dog, for she was growing frightened of him herself. She wished someone would come to help her.

Tommy was quite safe on his high perch but the dog would not give in. He barked and barked. Then he raised himself up on his hind legs and pawed against the scenery, trying to reach the cat.

"Get down from there!" cried Honey

Bunch, very much worried. "You're pawing mud all over Mr. Dare's scenery!"

The dog did not obey. To Honey Bunch's horror he knocked over one of the pieces of painted canvas, tearing a jagged hole in it with his sharp teeth. Tommy jumped down and darted out through the open door of the trailer.

For a moment the dog did not follow. Instead he sniffed at the cat's collar which had dropped to the floor. Then he picked it up in his teeth and raced outside.

"Drop that! You bad, bad dog!" cried Honey Bunch. "You drop that!"

By this time the commotion had brought Mr. and Mrs. Dare from the building.

"Just see what a big dog did to your scenery!" cried Honey Bunch. "I couldn't get him out of the trailer. And he took Tommy's collar!"

"I'll attend to him," said Mr. Dare grimly and ran out to find the dog.

Honey Bunch explained to Mrs. Dare just what had happened. She felt very sorry because the scenery had been damaged.

"I think we can mend the broken place," declared Mrs. Dare. "Don't worry about it, Honey Bunch."

By this time Tommy had disappeared. The little girl looked about the alley to see what had become of the cat. She was afraid it might be in danger. However, Mrs. Dare assured her that the animal knew how to take care of himself. He would come back to the trailer after the dog had gone away.

"Tommy often runs out and stays for an hour at a time," explained the puppet show lady. "But he always comes back."

Honey Bunch was standing in the doorway of the trailer when she heard someone call her name. Turning her head, she saw Norman running toward her.

"You better go straight home!" he shouted. "Mrs. Miller has looked almost everywhere for you!"

"Why, I've been here all the time," said Honey Bunch in surprise, for she hadn't dreamed anyone would be searching for her.

Norman was very happy to find that his

playmate had not been lost. He told her that
Ida and Mrs. Miller were looking for her too
and said again that she ought to hurry right
home.

"I'll have to go now," said the little girl to
Mrs. Dare. "Thank you for letting me see
your nice house on wheels."

"You are entirely welcome," smiled the
pretty lady. "Tell your mother we didn't realize anyone would be searching for you."

Honey Bunch said good-bye and went away
with Norman. The little fellow was a bit en-
vious because she had spent such a long while
inside the trailer.

"Anyway, I saw it too," he boasted.

"I helped Mr. Dare carry out the scenery,"
Honey Bunch explained. "Then Tommy—"

She stopped short, glancing back over her
shoulder. Norman halted too because he
couldn't imagine what was wrong.

"There's that big dog now!" exclaimed
Honey Bunch. "He's following us!"

"What dog, Honey Bunch?"

"Why, the one that tore a hole in Mr. Dare's

scenery. He came right into the trailer and tried to get Tommy—that's their cat. Oh, send him away, Norman."

"Sic 'em!" yelled Norman, making a little dart at the dog. "Go 'way! We don't want you tagging us home."

The dog stopped and stood eyeing the children. When they started on down the street, he followed behind them. Several times Norman and Honey Bunch drove him off, only to have him come after them again.

The animal was still following when they came within sight of the Morton house. They turned in at the front walk, and the dog turned in too just as if he lived there himself.

"Go away!" Norman ordered again. "We don't want you here."

Instead of leaving, the big dog began to bark. Honey Bunch saw then that her cat, Lady Clare, was lying on the front porch.

"Oh, Norman, do something quick!" she pleaded. "He's such a mean old dog! He'll hurt Lady Clare!"

CHAPTER IV

THE NEW TRAILER

NORMAN didn't know what to do because he really was afraid of the dog. Honey Bunch was so certain Lady Clare would be injured that she hurried to the porch and snatched the cat up in her arms. Even then the dog would not stop growling.

The little girl tried to open the front door but she couldn't get in. That was because Mrs. Miller always locked everything before she left the house. Honey Bunch didn't know what to do. Just at that moment she heard Norman, who had gone toward the street again, cry out:

"Honey Bunch, here comes Mrs. Miller now!"

The laundress was walking down the street very fast for she had seen the children.

"Oh, Mrs. Miller, this old dog is trying to

30

hurt Lady Clare," the little girl called.

The woman picked up a stick and switched the dog lightly on his hind legs. He went scooting out of the yard in a hurry.

"Honey Bunch, where have you been?" asked the laundress. "I've looked every place for you."

She was so relieved to see the little girl safe and sound that she gave her a big hug.

"Meow!" protested Lady Clare, who had been squeezed too.

"Honey Bunch was in the trailer," Norman declared. "I guess maybe you never would have found her if it hadn't been for me!"

"In a trailer!" exclaimed the laundress. "My goodness, what *will* you think of next? I've tramped the streets looking for you until I'm ready to drop."

Honey Bunch told Mrs. Miller that she was very sorry to have caused so much trouble. The laundress smiled when she heard how the little girl had wandered behind the stage to watch Mr. and Mrs. Dare, and then had followed them to their trailer house.

"I might have guessed it," declared Mrs. Miller. "You always were a child to learn what makes the wheels go 'round."

"Mr. and Mrs. Dare didn't use any wheels," said Honey Bunch earnestly. "They worked their puppets with strings."

Mrs. Miller laughed again, and told Honey Bunch that she hadn't actually meant wheels when she said that. It was just a way of saying that Honey Bunch was a curious child who liked to find out how things worked.

Before the laundress could unlock the front door, a car rolled up on the Morton driveway.

"There's my mother and my daddy!" cried Honey Bunch. She dropped Lady Clare and ran to meet her parents.

Mr. Morton assisted his wife from the automobile, then he swung his young daughter up onto his broad shoulder.

"Did you have a nice time today?" he asked her.

"Oh, yes, Daddy," declared his little girl. "Mrs. Miller took me to the puppet show."

"I'm very glad," returned her mother. "I

expected to take you there myself, but I had to
help Daddy so I couldn't get back in time.
What part did you like best, Honey Bunch?"

"The big red trailer! It was just wonderful! Daddy, I wish you would buy us one.
Then we could ride all over the country in it."

"I'd like that," laughed Mr. Morton. "But
don't you think we'd be crowded in a toy
trailer?"

"Oh, I mean a big moving house," insisted
Honey Bunch. "One large enough to hold you
and Mother and Mrs. Miller—"

Now Mrs. Miller, as you may remember,
was a very stout person. And then she had another idea, too, about the matter of a trailer.
"If I ever had a likin' for those boxed-up con-
traptions, it was taken out of me today."

She told Mrs. Morton how the little girl had
worried her by visiting Mr. Dare's "moving
house."

"Because of it your supper will be at least an
hour late," she added. "First the children
ruined all my baking, though I'll say it wasn't
exactly their fault. Then, when I should have

been cooking, I was out on the street trying to find Honey Bunch."

"I'm sure you've had a very trying day," said Mrs. Morton soothingly. "But there's no hurry about supper. Just take your time preparing it."

"I'll get it ready as fast as I can," promised Mrs. Miller, and went into the house.

It was now time for Norman to return to his own home. He didn't like to leave just then, for Honey Bunch and her parents were still talking about Mr. Dare's fine trailer.

"I've often wished we might spend a summer in one," said Mr. Morton thoughtfully. "It would be a pleasant way to see the country."

"Let's buy a trailer today, Daddy," pleaded Honey Bunch.

"Now don't tease, dear," chided her mother gently. "It would be fun to tour in a trailer, but I'm afraid we can't do it this year."

The next morning Norman came over the back fence to the Morton garden and called loudly for his playmate.

"Hey, Honey Bunch, I have something to show you," he cried. "Something important."

The little girl ran outside. Norman put his hand into a pocket and pulled out a shiny object. The little girl's eyes grew big as saucers.

Tommy cat's collar!

"Norman, wherever did you get that?" she gasped.

"I picked it up yesterday down by the Community Hall," he replied. "It's pretty nice. I thought I'd give it to Lady Clare for her birthday. When is Lady Clare's birthday?"

Honey Bunch didn't know just what to say. She thought it was very kind of Norman to want to remember her pet's birthday, but of course the collar must be returned to its owner.

"I'm sorry, Norman," she said at last, "but that beautiful collar belongs to Tommy, Mr. Dare's cat. The big dog that followed us yesterday took it out of the trailer. I thought the puppet man took it away from him."

"Let's go right down and give it to him," suggested the little boy a bit worried.

The children's parents said they might go

down town together, so off the two hurried.
When they reached the Community Hall, they
scooted through the alley to the parking lot at
the back.

It was empty!

"Oh!" cried Honey Bunch. "The Dares
have gone! And Tommy too!"

A janitor in the building told the little girl
and boy that the puppet show had moved to another town. He didn't know where.

"Now what'll I do?" Norman said later as
he and Honey Bunch walked toward home.

Suddenly the little fellow did the most unex-
pected thing. He started to laugh, then he got
down on the sidewalk and turned a somersault.

"Whatever is the matter with you, Norman
Clark?" asked his playmate.

"I know what I can do," said the little boy.
"My daddy's going to get a trailer, and we're
going on a trip, and I'll make them find the
puppet show, and I'll give the collar to
Tommy, and I'll—"

"You're going to do WHAT!" cried Honey
Bunch.

Norman was even more excited about trailers than Honey Bunch was, and he kept saying over and over that his parents were going to rent a moving house. Sure enough, one afternoon while the little girl was sitting on the porch with her mother and father, her playmate came running across the yard. He was almost out of breath.

"We've hired a big blue trailer!" Norman shouted. "Come over to our house and see it!"

Honey Bunch went with Norman right away. Her parents waited until Mrs. Clark came to the fence and asked them if they wouldn't like to see the new trailer too.

The Clarks' fine moving house which they had rented was much like Mr. Dare's trailer, except that it was blue instead of red.

"How cleverly everything has been arranged inside," declared Mrs. Morton. "So neat and compact. I do envy you, Mrs. Clark."

"Well, why not get a trailer of your own and come with us?" suggested Mrs. Clark. "We'd love that."

"Oh, Daddy, please do," pleaded Honey Bunch, tugging at her father's hand. "Mother wants to go and so do I!"

Mr. Morton didn't reply for a moment. He seemed to be thinking very hard about something.

"I'd enjoy the trip myself," he said slowly. "There's only one reason why I can't see my way clear to doing it. I must make a business trip to Fairhaven."

"Fairhaven?" inquired Mr. Clark. "Isn't that place located along the river in a summer resort district?"

"Yes, I believe it is."

"Then why couldn't we both travel to Fairhaven in trailers? One place is as good as another for us."

"I'm tempted to do it," Mr. Morton declared. "I really am. Let me think it over for a day."

"Think real hard, Daddy," Honey Bunch urged. "And then please say 'yes.' "

The next morning, Mr. Morton did say the magic word "yes." In the afternoon he took

Honey Bunch, her mother, and Norman to look at house trailers.

The children hadn't known there were so many trailers in the whole world. There were great big ones that looked almost like busses, and tiny ones which resembled playhouses.

While Mr. and Mrs. Morton talked to the salesmen, Norman and Honey Bunch climbed into the largest trailer they could find.

"Oh, isn't it grand?" the little girl said in awe as she looked around. "It's just like a little hotel."

When Norman did not answer, Honey Bunch wondered what he could be doing. She looked around to see. The little boy was tugging as hard as he could at a closet door.

"Be careful, Norman," she cautioned. "You know you promised your mother not to make any trouble."

"I'm not making trouble," replied Norman. "I'm just trying to open this door."

No matter how hard the little boy pulled, the closet door would not budge. Then he pushed sideways and it suddenly whirled around just like the revolving door in an office building.

"Oh, look!" Norman cried. "It's a merry-go-round door!"

"Isn't it funny?" laughed Honey Bunch. "You just turn it around and you can reach right in. And there are hooks to hang things on."

The children had never seen such a strange closet before. It really was two little wardrobes in one. They turned the door slowly around.

First one tiny section whirled past, then another. After that the door appeared again. Norman pulled a latch on the knob and something clicked.

"Now see what you've done, Norman," said Honey Bunch in dismay. "The closet is locked up."

"That's nothing," boasted Norman. "I can unlock it just as easy as anything."

The little boy pulled the latch again and the door opened. Then he whirled the closet real hard. Before Honey Bunch knew what he was doing, Norman had stepped into one of the little sections.

The closet turned around with him in it. Then suddenly the latch to the door snapped shut. He was locked inside.

"Let me out!" cried Norman. "I'm smothering!"

Honey Bunch worked hard at the latch but she could not open it, though she pinched her finger several times trying to do so.

"It's dark in here," cried Norman. "Hurry up or I'll go blind."

The little girl kept tugging at the door and all the time Norman became more and more frightened. Honey Bunch could hear him sobbing and beating the wall with his hands.

"I'll run and get Daddy!" she called to encourage him.

Honey Bunch found her mother and father talking with the salesman.

"Come quick!" she cried. "Norman locked himself in the closet. He's smothering and thinks he's going blind."

CHAPTER V

A STOWAWAY

THE grown-ups hurried to the trailer. In a moment Norman was free again. His face was wet with tears and Mrs. Morton gently wiped them away. He sat down in a chair and did not look at any more of the big coaches.

After Mr. Morton had talked some more with the salesman, he decided to buy a nice looking red trailer. Honey Bunch was glad that it had an ordinary wardrobe closet and not one which revolved.

"After your trip you'll have no trouble in selling such a fine trailer as this one," the salesman told Mr. Morton.

"What shall we name our new house on wheels?" Mrs. Morton asked the children.

"Let's call it the *Robin*," said Honey Bunch quickly. "It's red like one."

"That is a very good name, dear," smiled her mother.

"And we'll call our trailer the *Bluebird*," declared Norman Clark. "Because it's blue and white just like a bluebird."

After that the two trailers were called the *Robin* and the *Bluebird*. Norman thought the blue trailer the better one just because it belonged to his family. Honey Bunch didn't mind. For herself she liked the *Robin*.

The next few days were busy ones indeed. The children helped store away things in the drawers and closets of the trailer. But many articles had to be left behind.

"Mother, where will Lady Clare sleep?" asked Honey Bunch anxiously.

"I'm afraid we can't take the cat with us," replied Mrs. Morton. "Lady Clare will have to stay with Mrs. Miller."

Honey Bunch felt disappointed. She had counted upon having Lady Clare with her.

"A cat would be very much of a nuisance in a trailer," explained Mother gently. "Hilda will keep you from being lonesome." Hilda was Honey Bunch's favorite doll.

Mrs. Miller promised that she would take

good care of the cat while the Mortons were
gone. The laundress was very busy these days
for there was a great deal of work to be done
before the family should start away in their
trailer.

Honey Bunch tried to be as helpful as she
could. When Mrs. Miller hung up the wash
the little girl handed up the clothespins.

"Thank you, Honey Bunch," the laundress
smiled. She took a pin the little girl had given
her and used it to fasten a pair of play overalls
to the line.

"Oh, that's mine," Honey Bunch said. "I'm
taking it with me on the trailer trip. Were the
overalls hard to get clean, Mrs. Miller?"

"Land sakes, yes," the laundress sighed. "I
don't see how you get your clothes so soiled."

"I do," the little girl laughed. "I'm a roller
skater."

"You must do your roller skating sitting
down!" laughed the woman.

"Well, I do fall down sometimes," Honey
Bunch admitted. "Everyone does except Ida
Camp. She's the best skater on our street."

"She must be an expert," Mrs. Miller said as she picked up the last garment in the basket.

"What is an expert, Mrs. Miller?" Whenever the little girl heard a new word she always asked its meaning because she was eager to learn things.

"Well, an expert is one who knows how to do a thing well."

"Oh, I see," Honey Bunch answered slowly. "You are an expert wash lady. Ida is an expert skater. And I am an expert—what *am* I expert at, Mrs. Miller? Oh, I know! I'm an expert ice cream eater!"

Mrs. Miller laughed and agreed that Honey Bunch was very good at eating ice cream. Then she picked up the basket and went into the house.

Both Honey Bunch and Norman counted the days until they could start on the trailer trip. They did not see very much of each other, so the little girl did not know that her playmate was going to take his harmonica with him.

Then at last they were ready to leave for

Fairhaven. The children picked garden flowers and decorated the *Robin* and the *Bluebird* so that the trailers looked very gay and cheerful. Many neighbors came to see the Clarks and the Mortons make their start.

"Have a good time," called Mrs. Miller when the cars were ready to pull away with their trailers behind them. "I'll look after everything here."

The Mortons drove ahead, moving slowly because of the heavy load.

"Daddy, won't we go any faster than this?" Honey Bunch asked. She was afraid it would take them a long while to reach Fairhaven.

"We'll speed up after we are out of town," her father promised her. "I haven't the feel of the wheel yet."

"You don't like to blow your own horn, do you?" the little girl wanted to know.

Daddy Morton laughed. "If you mean on the car, no, I don't. One ought to drive well enough so he doesn't have to use his horn very often."

"I don't mean that," said Honey Bunch.

"Mrs. Miller says if you toot your own horn it's boasting, and boasting isn't nice."

"She's right," added Mother. "It's much better to be modest and not boast."

"But Mrs. Miller says," went on the little girl, "that sometimes you have to toot your own horn a little bit to let people know what you can do."

Just at that moment a dog ran right in front of the car and Daddy Morton tooted the car horn very loudly. The animal hustled out of the way.

Honey Bunch giggled. "I guess you had to boast that time, didn't you, Daddy?"

At the next corner both trailers turned into a filling station. While the attendant was working the gasoline pump, Mr. Morton went back to see how the *Robin* was riding. Of course Honey Bunch jumped from the car and went with him.

"Everything seems to be all right," declared Mr. Morton.

Honey Bunch stood with her ear close to the door of the trailer.

"Daddy, what is that funny sound?" she asked. "I think someone is hiding in our trailer!"

"I don't believe anyone is inside the trailer," declared Mr. Morton.

He opened the door and looked into the spic and span interior. No one was hiding there.

"But Daddy," protested Honey Bunch. "I'm sure I heard something."

"What sort of a noise?"

"It went 'scratch, scratch,' just like a big rat."

Mr. Morton listened for a moment but he did not hear any sound.

"Perhaps you were mistaken," he said. "I'm sure there are no rats or mice in our new trailer."

The gasoline station man had finished filling the tank of the car, so Mr. Morton went back to pay him. They drove off and Honey Bunch forgot about the noise which she had heard in the trailer.

That is, she did for the time being. But at twelve o'clock, when the *Robin* and the *Blue-*

bird pulled up in a shady dell for luncheon, the little girl was certain she heard the sound once more. While she helped her mother string beans, she listened closely.

"There it is again, Mother," she said. "Don't you hear it?"

"Why yes, I do notice a soft, scratching sound."

Mrs. Morton bent down and peered under the couch.

"Is it a big rat?" asked Honey Bunch anxiously. She knew rats caused lots of damage.

Mother began to laugh. And then Honey Bunch understood why, because out scooted Lady Clare from under the couch.

"Why, Lady Clare, how did you get here?" cried the little girl.

She was so glad to see her pet that she caught the adorable black cat in her arms and gave her a big hug.

"Honey Bunch, you didn't hide Lady Clare in the trailer?" asked Mother.

"Oh, no," said her little daughter. "I thought she was back home with Mrs. Miller."

"I suppose the cat must have managed to get into the trailer when the door was left open. We'll write Mrs. Miller at once. She'll be worried if she thinks the animal ran away and got lost."

"May Lady Clare go with us to Fairhaven?" Honey Bunch inquired eagerly.

"I'm afraid it's too late to send her home," sighed Mrs. Morton. "Yes, your cat played a joke on us this time."

Honey Bunch took her beautiful pet in her arms and ran to the *Bluebird* to tell Norman of her discovery. The little boy had gone to a nearby spring for a jug of water, but he soon came back. Without even noticing the cat, he cried:

"Honey Bunch, there's another trailer camped up by the spring! Bet you can't guess whose it is!"

"Mr. Dare's?"

"How did you know?" Norman was disappointed because Honey Bunch had guessed so easily.

"I just hoped it might be," laughed the little girl. "Now you can return Tommy's collar to him."

Norman carried the water to the *Bluebird,* where he got the collar with the pretty red stones out of a drawer. Then he and Honey Bunch raced off to visit Mr. and Mrs. Dare.

While Tommy and Lady Clare frolicked together with a ball of twine, the little girl told the couple about how her cat had hidden in the *Robin.*

"Kitties are very smart," declared Mrs. Dare. "I think Lady Clare wanted to go on a trailer trip."

It was a great surprise when Norman took the collar from his pocket and told how he had found it and how he and Honey Bunch had tried to return it.

"Oh, you precious boy!" cried Mrs. Dare. "That is a valuable collar and I was sure it was lost forever."

Now Norman was glad of the praise, but he didn't like to be called "precious." He prided himself on being a real he-boy and he thought "precious" sounded kind of sissy.

After a while the children took the couple to meet their parents. The grown-ups seemed to like each other very much for they talked and talked.

"Are you staying here long?" Mr. Morton asked them.

"That all depends upon how folks like our show," the man answered. "We're heading for Fairhaven."

"That's where we're going!" cried Honey Bunch in delight.

Soon the Dares went back to their trailer. The Mortons and the Clarks decided to remain at this pleasant spot for the rest of the day. After luncheon Honey Bunch helped with the dishes, then she and Norman ran over to the Dare trailer. The puppet show man was sitting under a shade tree, sorting out his marionettes.

"Hello, Honey Bunch," he said. "Your cat just did me a good turn."

"Why, has Lady Clare been over here again?" asked Honey Bunch.

Mr. Dare nodded and showed the children

where a piece had been chewed out of one of
his nicest puppets.

"Lady Clare didn't do that?" Honey Bunch
gasped.

"No, I carelessly left some of my puppets
lying out here under the tree. Field mice
started to chew them. I'd not have noticed if
Lady Clare and Tommy hadn't gone into ac-
tion."

"What did the cats do?" asked Norman.

"They chased the pests away," replied Mr.
Dare. "We gave Lady Clare and Tommy
some choice morsels of food as their reward."

Honey Bunch felt very proud that her kitty
had been of such service. She and Norman
wandered into the trailer to talk with Mrs.
Dare. After a while they came outside again,
Mr. Dare had gone away somewhere.

He had left the box of puppets standing by
the tree. Norman picked up the Prince.

"Let's play puppets," he teased Honey
Bunch. "It will be fun with real dolls. You
be the Princess."

"We shouldn't without asking," Honey

Bunch said doubtfully. "We might hurt the dolls."

"Oh, Mr. Dare won't care," Norman returned.

"Please put the 'Prince' back in the box," Honey Bunch pleaded.

"All right, in just a minute. I want to show it to those boys over there."

Before the little girl could stop him, Norman took the puppet and went off to talk with three strange boys who were staring curiously at the *Bluebird*. They were several years older than Norman and he wanted to impress them.

"That's our big blue trailer," he said boastfully. "My daddy owns it."

"Oh, we've seen lots better trailers!" scoffed one of the boys. "Look, fellows! The kid still plays with dolls!"

"I don't either," cried Norman angrily. "This is a puppet. Mr. Dare uses it in his show."

"Let me see it," said the boy.

He took the Prince roughly from Norman's

hand. The boys passed the doll around among them and then they turned as if to walk away.

"Give me back my Prince," said Norman, following them.

"Oh, you don't want this doll any more," teased one of the boys. "We'll keep it for you."

"I do too want it!" cried Norman angrily. "It belongs to Mr. Dare."

The boys paid no attention but walked off into the woods. Norman knew that he never could get the puppet by himself. He ran back toward the trailer, shouting for Mrs. Dare to come. The woman did not hear, for she had taken her market basket and gone to a nearby grocery store.

"Mother! Daddy!" called the little boy.

His parents and the Mortons were enjoying a tramp along the lake. They were too far away to be of aid. Honey Bunch was the only person to hear Norman's cry. She ran toward him.

"Oh, Honey Bunch, those mean boys ran off with the Prince," Norman told her tearfully.

"I asked them to give it back but they just laughed."

"Which way did they go?" asked the little girl.

"Into the woods."

"Then we must go right after them," declared Honey Bunch. "Mr. Dare never will be able to give another puppet show without the Prince. We just have to get him back, Norman!"

CHAPTER VI

HENRY'S GOAT

THE children ran as fast as they could after the three older boys who had carried away the puppet. They soon caught sight of them.

"Wait!" called Norman. "Give us back the Prince!"

The lads paused, but when Norman reached out to take the doll, it was held high above his head.

"Oh, please, you don't understand," pleaded Honey Bunch. "The Prince belongs to Mr. Dare."

"What will you give us to get it back?" teased the boy who had the doll.

Norman searched through his pockets and found an agate marble.

"You'll have to give me more than that if you want the doll back," said the mean boy.

Norman couldn't find anything of value in his pocket, but Honey Bunch remembered a

57

dime which was tied up in her handkerchief.
Mrs. Miller had given it to her for ice cream
but she had saved it. She hated to part with
the money, but they just had to get back Mr.
Dare's puppet.

"Will you give us the Prince if I pay you
ten cents?" she asked.

"Let's see your money."

Honey Bunch shook her head. She was
afraid the boy might take the dime away from
her too.

"Let me have the puppet first," she insisted.
"Then I'll give you the money."

"Oh, all right," agreed the boy after a moment. "Here is your old doll. I didn't want
it anyway."

He tossed the Prince into Honey Bunch's
arms. The little girl meant to keep her bar-
gain so she started to undo the hard knot in
her handkerchief.

"Never mind the money," said the boy
gruffly. He was a bit ashamed of himself now.
"Keep it." With his companions he turned
and walked into the woods.

Honey Bunch and Norman were very happy to have the puppet again. They hurried as fast as they could with it back to camp.

During their absence Mr. and Mrs. Dare had returned to their trailer and found that the Prince was missing. They were beginning to grow alarmed when the children came running up with the marionette.

"Oh, so you went walking with the Prince," declared Mr. Dare, greatly relieved. "That doll is worth fifty dollars. I was afraid it might have been stolen."

Norman had not dreamed that the puppet was so valuable. He made up his mind he would never borrow anything again without asking the owner's permission to do so.

Mr. Dare did not scold the little boy, but he was careful to put all his puppets away inside the trailer. His wife began packing up also.

"Are you leaving camp?" asked Honey Bunch as she helped gather up a few things.

"Yes, we'll probably pull out early in the morning," replied Mr. Dare. "Our show was good for only a one-day stand here."

"I hope we see you again," said the little girl wistfully.

"We'll miss you too, you dear children," declared Mrs. Dare, giving them each a squeeze. Norman grew red in the face, for he didn't like this. "But perhaps we'll meet again on the road some fine day," the woman continued.

The following morning the Mortons and the Clarks got ready to leave. Honey Bunch and Norman begged to be allowed to ride together in the *Robin*.

"We'd like to play keeping house by ourselves," said the little girl. "Norman's my brother and he has to go on a business trip."

"I'll be too grown-up to get in mischief," announced Norman, when he saw his mother look at his daddy in a queer sort of way.

Permission was finally given and with cries of joy the playmates were locked in the *Robin* and the two families started off.

"I have to work on some papers," said Norman importantly, making his voice deep like his daddy's. "You get the lunch."

Honey Bunch never had a brother but she

didn't think she'd like one if he were going to be so bossy. But she looked in the trailer icebox and found some eggs, some milk and some fruit.

"I b'lieve I'll make a banana pudding like Mrs. Miller does," she thought.

While she was busy, her daddy and mother rode along comfortably in their car, wondering what the children were doing.

"I hope they're all right," said Mrs. Morton. "I'm just a little worried. Oh—!"

Her husband had to put his foot on the brake quickly, for a car had come out of a side road right in front of them. At the same time the Mortons heard a scream.

"Oh, the children!" gasped Honey Bunch's mother.

She hurried back to the trailer. The little boy and girl were all right, but what a mess the *Robin* was. White and yellow fluid from eggs was running along the floor. Milk was splashed on the couch, the table and the children's clothes. Slices of bananas were lying everywhere.

"My goodness!" exclaimed Mrs. Morton. Norman and Honey Bunch felt very bad, but Daddy Morton said he thought he was as much to blame as anyone, for as he had stopped the car quickly the food had fallen over.

The Clarks had come up, of course, and they helped to clean up the *Robin*.

After a long silence Honey Bunch said, "Many hands make light work." Everyone laughed, for they knew the little girl had heard Mrs. Miller use that grown-up expression often.

"Now we better hurry along," said Daddy Morton, so the travelers went on their way again.

At nightfall camp was made near the outskirts of a town in a large tourist park. In a very short time a small colored lad, grinning broadly, came to the door of the *Robin*. He had some boxes of blackberries for sale.

"Two fo' a qua'ter, Ma'am," he told Mrs. Morton, politely sweeping off his straw hat. "Dese is nice berries. Dey come from my pappy's own farm."

"They look lovely," said Mrs. Morton.

While she was searching for her pocketbook, Honey Bunch and Norman appeared. The little girl liked the way the colored boy grinned so she smiled back at him and said:

"What's your name?"

"Henry Black."

"Where do you live?" asked Norman, because he wanted to get acquainted with the colored boy too and sample some of his food if possible.

"Back up on de hill a ways," Henry answered. "If you all will come home with me, Ah'll show you mah goat."

"Oh, that would be a lot of fun," said Honey Bunch. "I'll ask Mother."

When Mrs. Morton came to pay Henry for the berries the little girl asked her if she might go with the colored lad to see his goat.

"Why yes, if you like," agreed Mother. "But don't stay long."

Mr. Clark said that Norman might go along too, so the children started off with Henry. The colored boy's home was in plain view of both trailers. It was a rickety old cabin at the edge of a wood. There was a small fenced-in yard just in front. The goat was eating grass near the gate.

"Oh, he's a nice fat fellow," said Norman, leaning on the rails of the fence. "What's his name?"

"It's a girl goat," Henry replied. "Her name is Nanny Can."

"Nanny Can," repeated Honey Bunch. "Why do you call her by that name?"

"I reckon it's 'cause she's fond o' tin cans. Dat goat tries to eat everything around. You all just wait heah. Ah's goin' for a cup."

Henry went into the cabin and soon returned with a large cup.

"Would you all like some goat milk?" he asked with his widest smile. "It won't hurt you none. It tastes good and 'sides dat, goat milk is lucky, so mah Pappy says."

"Why?" inquired Honey Bunch eagerly.

"Everything 'bout a goat is lucky," answered Henry. "Mebbe that's 'cause they's not afraid of anything."

He stooped down and held the cup under Nanny Can. The milk went zing! zing! into the tin until soon it was nearly full. Honey Bunch and Norman drank some of it but they didn't like it as well as plain old fashioned cow's milk. Of course, they were too polite to say so, for they didn't wish to hurt Henry's feelings.

"You see," explained Henry later, "Nanny Can an' me ain't 'fraid of nothin' but lightning an' ghosts."

"Do you have scarey white ghosts around here?" asked Norman, looking hastily over his shoulders, first to the right and then to the left.

"Deed we do," continued the colored boy. "I saw one. It was awful. It came after us even."

"Oho," laughed Honey Bunch, "you're just trying to tease us. There are no real ghosts— just people dressing up on Hallowe'en in bed sheets or something like that."

"You jest wait and see," muttered Henry. "You jest wait and see. Me and Nanny Can know."

Norman and Honey Bunch had promised their parents they would not stay away long, so they now told Henry good-bye.

"I wish we had a goat to take with us in the trailer," remarked Norman as the two walked back to camp.

"A goat would be too much trouble on such a trip," replied Honey Bunch, "Nanny Can wouldn't compact very well."

"You mean *pack*," corrected Norman.

"Why, anyone knows you can't pack a goat!" Honey Bunch returned quickly. "I've heard my mother say lots of times that things which go into a trailer must be small and compact."

It was nearly supper time when the children reached camp. Honey Bunch set the table as she did for each meal. Norman had chores of his own to attend to. After the evening meal the children played under the trees for a while until it was bedtime. Norman secretly kept watch in case a queer white figure should spring out from behind a tall tree. But none did. Finally the playmates told each other good night.

Honey Bunch went right off to sleep for she was very tired. Usually the little girl slept through till morning, but tonight was different. She suddenly found herself wide awake.

It was very dark in the trailer. Honey Bunch would have felt afraid if she hadn't known her parents were sleeping near by.

The little girl lay perfectly still, listening. She was certain some strange sound had awakened her. For a moment she thought Lady Clare must be stirring about in the trailer.

But a cat would not make such a loud noise. There it was again.

Knock! Knock! This time Honey Bunch knew she was not dreaming.

"Someone must be at the door," thought the little girl.

She jumped out of bed and padded across the floor. Honey Bunch shivered because it was chilly, and, well, she was a bit afraid.

Tiptoeing to the oval window, she peered outside to see who was at the door. No one was there.

At that moment the little girl happened to

glance toward the Clark trailer. She was startled to see something large and white and very much alive leaping about among the trees.

"Mother! Daddy!" cried Honey Bunch. "There's a ghost outside our trailer!"

CHAPTER VII

HONEY BUNCH'S "GHOST."

DADDY MORTON was sleeping soundly, but he awoke instantly and sat up in bed.

"What is the matter?" he asked drowsily. "Honey Bunch, why are you standing there by the window?"

"Daddy, there's a big g-ghost outside!" cried Honey Bunch. She was so excited it was hard for her not to stutter. "He knocked on our door. Now he's trying to get into the *Bluebird!*"

"Nonsense!" returned her father. "There are no ghosts, Honey Bunch. You must have had a dream. Hop right back into bed."

"Daddy, you can *see* him!"

By this time Mrs. Morton was awake too. Both she and her husband went over to the window just to satisfy Honey Bunch.

"Why, there *is* something white moving about!" exclaimed Mrs. Morton.

"It's a g-ghost!" insisted Honey Bunch.

"The thing does look like one," admitted Daddy Morton. "But it couldn't be. I'll find out what it is!"

He put on his shoes and a long coat and went out into the cold night. Even though she was frightened, Honey Bunch just had to giggle, because her daddy looked very funny chasing a ghost.

For a time it seemed as if Mr. Morton couldn't get very close to the darting white object. It would run first in one direction and then another, until finally it butted its head right against a tree.

That gave Mr. Morton his chance. He reached out and seized the ghost. Then both Honey Bunch and her mother had to laugh. It wasn't a ghost at all, but a goat! A goat with a white shirt over its head.

Mr. Morton came hurrying back to the *Robin* with the tattered garment in his hand. He had driven the goat off toward the hill.

"Daddy, that must have been Nanny Can," observed Honey Bunch.

"How in the world could a goat have got its head into a shirt?" asked Mrs. Morton. She was weak from laughter.

"Must have run through a clothesline," replied Mr. Morton. "Our ghost mystery is solved."

He tucked Honey Bunch back into her warm bed but the little girl couldn't go to sleep right away. She kept listening, wondering if Henry Black's goat would come to visit the trailer again.

Soon her eyes grew heavy and she went off to dreamland. When she awakened it was morning. Her mother said that the goat had not returned during the night.

As soon as she was dressed Honey Bunch ran to tell Norman about the ghost. The little boy was very much put out because he had missed all the excitement.

"I'm s'prised you couldn't tell a goat, Honey Bunch," he said in a superior tone.

"But the goat had a shirt over its head. I don't believe you could have told a goat from a ghost either, Norman."

"I bet you thought it was Henry Black's ghost and were awful scared."

"No, I wasn't either," protested the little girl.

"Sure you were," teased Norman. "All girls are fraid cats. If I had been awake I would have gone right out, an'—"

In his excitement the little boy did not watch where he was walking. He stumbled, and as luck would have it, in trying to save himself from falling, he put his hand right into a bees' nest.

"Run, Norman! Run!" shouted Honey Bunch excitedly.

She darted away like a flash. But the little boy wasn't quick enough. Honey Bunch heard him cry out in pain and alarm as he was stung on the leg.

"Oh, are you hurt?" she called anxiously, and ran back to help him.

Norman was holding fast to his leg with both hands. Tears were in his eyes.

"It hurts awful," he said with a sob in his voice.

"If you can walk back to the trailer, Mother will put something on it," Honey Bunch said encouragingly.

Norman walked a few steps, then sat down on a log.

"I'll run and get Mother," Honey Bunch said kindly.

Before she could leave the children heard a sound in the bushes. Out stepped Henry Black. Honey Bunch told the colored boy how Norman had been stung by a bumble bee.

"Wheah 'bouts he light on you?" Henry Black asked. He grinned as if he thought being stung by a bee wasn't anything to cry about.

"On my leg," said Norman. "See, it's swelling up."

"You is lucky," laughed the colored boy. "Dem bumble bees mostly goes right fo' your eyes. I remembers de time when one closed up both mah eyes so tight Ah couldn't see."

"That must have hurt awful, Henry," Honey Bunch said.

"It sho' did, Missy. Ah felt so miserable Ah couldn't eat."

"There, you see, Norman," Honey Bunch said. "You're really not hurt much. Not like Henry was, anyhow."

"Mud packs is good fo' a leg sting," said Henry. "You just wait here, Norman. Ah'll make you one."

The colored boy scooped up a handful of clay and carried it down to a little brook. He mixed the clay with water and plastered it on the swollen leg.

"How dat feel now?" he asked.

Norman had to admit that the mud pack took away nearly all the pain.

"Henry, did your goat run off last night?" Honey Bunch asked after the children had talked a few minutes.

"Nanny Can busted loose from her rope. Dat ole goat ripped down de clothesline and ran off with pappy's best white shirt."

"We have the shirt," said Honey Bunch. "Only it's all torn to pieces."

"Ah bettah get it anyway," declared Henry. "Mah pappy don't own no other white one."

The colored boy walked back to the trailer

with the children. When Mrs. Morton showed him the tattered shirt, he saw right away that it never could be used again. One sleeve was gone and there was a long tear all the way down the front.

"Ah don't know what my pappy will do now," he said sadly. "He cain't nevah go to chu'ch no mo' without a shirt."

Honey Bunch felt sorry that the goat had made so much trouble. She did not see how Henry's father could get along without his shirt. And of course he did not have any money to buy another for he was such a poor man. Just then the little girl saw Mr. Morton coming toward the trailer.

"Oh, I have an idea!" she cried. "Wait here, Henry."

Honey Bunch ran to meet her daddy. She told him all about the shirt problem.

"Couldn't you give Henry's father one of your old shirts?" she pleaded. "Then he could go to church again."

"Now that's an idea," laughed Mr. Morton. "I'll see what I can find."

He went into the *Robin* and looked through his wardrobe. Soon he came back, carrying a clean white shirt which had never been taken from its store wrapper and gave it to his little daughter.

"Here is a new one for your father, Henry," said Honey Bunch as she presented her father's gift to the waiting lad.

"Thank you, thank you. Ah knew dat goat would bring us good luck!" Henry's lips parted in a big broad grin. He took the package and ran up the hill.

Honey Bunch and Norman were sorry when their parents decided it was time to leave this spot. But late afternoon found both trailers camped in a pleasant site by a small waterfall.

"Mother, may I go wading in the river?" pleaded Honey Bunch. "Norman has his shoes off."

"Why yes," Mrs. Morton agreed. "I'll sit on the steps of the trailer and watch you."

Norman and Honey Bunch had fun splashing in the shallow water. Soon the little boy grew daring and went close to the waterfall.

The stream of water fell from a rocky ledge. Right behind it was a small space where one could see the rocks.

"Bet I could walk right under there and never get one speck wet!" boasted Norman.

"Let's try it!" cried Honey Bunch. "It will be fun."

Mrs. Morton arose and came closer to the waterfall. She said nothing to the children for she decided that they would be in no danger if they did try to walk under the falls. If they slipped they might get a ducking, but the water was shallow and therefore safe.

"Let me go first!" cried Honey Bunch, holding her play suit tight against her.

She squeezed flat beside the ledge and moved an inch at a time along the rocks.

"I can feel the spray on my face!" shouted the little girl. "But I'm not getting wet!"

"This is fun," cried Norman, who was right behind his playmate. "Come in with us, Mrs. Morton."

"The opening would be too small for me," laughed Honey Bunch's mother.

"Oh, I can't go any farther," called her little daughter suddenly, "or I'll get wet."

"Then come back, dear," advised Mrs. Morton. "I really feel uneasy for fear you'll tumble into the water."

Honey Bunch could not turn around for there wasn't room enough. She had to back very slowly, and as she looked down to see where she was tramping, her eyes fastened upon an object lying on the ledge. She hadn't noticed it before because it was so dark behind the spray of water.

"Norman, look what I've found!" she exclaimed.

She stooped and picked up a small leather pouch.

"How can I look when you're standing right in front of me?" demanded Norman. "What did you find, Honey Bunch?"

"A little leather bag! It's heavy, too."

The children were very excited by this time. They backed slowly from behind the falls. Honey Bunch held up the leather bag for her mother to see.

"Why, it is a little pouch with a draw string!" exclaimed Mrs. Morton. "Someone may have hidden it behind the waterfall. Let me see it, dear."

She took the bag from the little girl's outstretched hand. The children crowded close to watch her open it. Mrs. Morton pulled the string and reached her hand down into the pouch. She drew out a gold bracelet.

"Jewelry!" she gasped.

Mrs. Morton sat down on the creek bank and emptied the contents of the bag into her lap. Besides the bracelet there were rings, a locket, earrings and other articles of jewelry. Nearly every piece was set with sparkling stones.

Mrs. Morton was almost as excited as the children. She called Honey Bunch's daddy and Norman's parents. The grown-ups all agreed that the jewelry was very valuable.

"This is a find," commented Norman's father, turning the gold pieces over and over.

"I wonder how it happened to be in that niche behind the waterfall?" speculated Mrs. Clark.

"It may be stolen jewelry," declared Mr. Morton. "Possibly the thief was afraid to sell it and hid it here."

"Or it could have been left there by the real owner," added Mrs. Morton.

"Will we keep the jewelry?" asked Honey Bunch, trying on a bracelet.

"No, dear," replied her mother, "not if we are able to find the rightful owner. But it may be hard to locate that person."

"Maybe whoever hid the jewelry will come back for it," said Honey Bunch.

"Just what I was thinking," nodded Mr. Morton. "We could remove the jewels from the case and put the pouch back under the waterfall. Then we could watch for the person to return."

The others agreed that the idea was a very good one. Mr. Morton could not reach very far into the niche. Honey Bunch crept back under the falls, and placed the leather bag exactly where she had found it.

"Will the owner come for it tonight, do you think, Daddy?" she asked.

"He may, and then he may not come for weeks," replied Mr. Morton. "We'll just camp here a while and see what does happen."

"Let me stay up all night and watch!" teased Norman.

"No, we'll all go to bed," answered his father. "If anyone appeared to be around, the person might not come."

"Mr. Clark and I will sleep with one eye open," promised Mr. Morton. "If anyone approaches the camp, we'll be certain to see him."

Honey Bunch wondered how her father could sleep with one eye open. She decided that it was just a saying which meant that he would try to keep awake.

"Norman, let's keep our eyes open too," she told her playmate. "Maybe that jewelry man will come back tonight!"

CHAPTER VIII

A BAG OF JEWELS

HONEY BUNCH and Norman were unable to stay awake very long after they went to bed. In the morning their parents told them that no one had come near the waterfall during the night.

"I didn't really expect anyone so soon," declared Mr. Morton. "We'll watch for several days and nights."

The camp site was a delightful one. The men brought fish which they caught in the stream. Honey Bunch and Norman would go for tramps through the woods with their mothers. Someone always remained at camp to keep watch, though.

Several days after Honey Bunch's find Mr. Morton put an advertisement in the newspaper of the nearby town. In it he asked that the person who owned the leather bag get in touch

with him. Of course, he was wise enough not
to tell what had been found in the pouch. No
answer came and he was very disappointed.

"I thought surely we would find the owner,"
he declared. "Still, someone may come if we
wait a few days longer."

Honey Bunch and Norman seldom went far
from camp. They liked to remain within sight
of the waterfall. One day, however, they wandered a long way down the river.

Honey Bunch was sailing a birch bark boat
when she happened to glance up. A short
distance away she saw an old man with a long
red beard. He was scooping up a bucket of
water from the stream.

The stranger did not see the children at first.
He started to walk away from the brook, but
stopped as Norman and Honey Bunch ran toward him.

"Hello," said the little girl. "Can we help
you? Do you live near here?" she asked.

The old man stared at her. "Yes, little girl,"
he answered gravely. "I live back in the
woods."

"Have you any little girls or boys?" questioned Norman.

The old man shook his head. He told the children he lived alone. "Folks call me a hermit," he added bitterly.

"We live in a trailer," Honey Bunch said proudly. Then, remembering about the leather bag found behind the waterfall, she asked, "Have you lost anything?"

"Everything in the world," the hermit replied in a sad voice. "Everything."

Norman and Honey Bunch looked quickly at each other. Their parents had warned them to be very cautious in speaking of the bag of jewelry. They didn't dare come right out and ask the old man if he had lost the pouch, yet they felt somehow that it must belong to him.

The hermit with the red beard started to walk away with his bucket of water, but Norman ran after him.

"Let me help you," said the little fellow.

"No, no, I must go alone," said the old man wearily.

"Have you a secret you're keeping?" the boy

asked. He wanted to ask many more questions.

"Yes," replied the hermit, very low. "A heavy burden lies upon my heart."

Without even glancing at Norman he moved off into the woods.

"You see!" cried the boy after the old man was beyond hearing. "He has a secret, Honey Bunch. He said so."

"Maybe we should have told him about finding the bag of jewelry."

The hermit was far away by this time. The children knew they could never overtake him in the dense woods.

"Let's run back to camp and tell Mother!" urged Honey Bunch.

The two children hurried as fast as they could to the waterfall. Mr. Morton and Mr. Clark had just returned from a fishing trip, and promised that they would set out again in search of the hermit.

"I doubt that the jewelry belongs to that old man," said Mr. Morton, "but he may have seen the person who hid the bag. We'll question him about it."

The children went with their fathers, showing them where last they had seen the hermit. The party tramped into the woods but could find no sign of any cabin or of the old man who might live in it.

"We may as well give up," said Mr. Morton finally. "Let's start back to camp. We've gone a great deal farther than I thought," declared Mr. Morton anxiously.

"We're not lost, are we, Daddy?" asked Honey Bunch.

"Oh, no," said her father lightly. "We're not lost. It's the camp which is missing!"

The children laughed as they all walked on. It was growing dark in the woods. Black clouds scudded overhead.

"I hope it doesn't rain," said Daddy Morton.

The tall tree tops were waving and bending in the breeze. Honey Bunch wished they could get back to camp right away.

"We're in for a storm, all right," declared Mr. Clark as he stepped over a fallen tree branch.

Honey Bunch could hear the roar of the wind. Or was it the wind?

"Daddy, listen!" she cried. "I hear our waterfall!"

Both men stopped and listened intently.

"You're right, my dear!" exclaimed Mr. Morton. He was so relieved he laughed aloud. "Now I know where we are."

The men followed the sound made by the splashing water. In a few minutes they were all safe in camp. Scarcely had they closed themselves into the snug trailers when the rain came down in torrents.

In the morning the river had overflowed its banks. Honey Bunch was glad when her daddy put on his rubber coat and with a long stick rescued the leather pouch from behind the waterfall. She was afraid it might be washed away.

"We should be starting for Fairhaven," declared Mr. Morton. "I don't dare waste any more time on the road."

The jewelry was stored in the *Robin*. Both trailers then journeyed on toward the summer resort city. By nightfall the Mortons and the Clarks were situated pleasantly in an attractive tourist park on a lake.

Honey Bunch and Norman set off together to explore their surroundings. They had not gone far when they came to a tree which bore a bright red poster.

"Oh, see, Norman!" cried Honey Bunch. "It's an advertisement of Mr. Dare's puppet show!"

"Maybe the show is here now!"

The children looked at the date on the poster.

"It says the twenty-fourth," read Honey Bunch. "What date is this, Norman?"

"Why, the twenty-fourth. The puppet show was held in Fairhaven today."

"Maybe Mr. and Mrs. Dare are still here anyway," said Honey Bunch hopefully. "Let's look at all the trailers."

The children started at one corner of the park and looked at every vehicle. There were rows and rows of trailers. Some were new and shiny like the *Robin* and the *Bluebird*. Others

"OH!" CRIED HONEY BUNCH, "MAYBE THE SHOW IS HERE NOW!"

were old. Norman and Honey Bunch had never imagined so many trailers would come to one spot at one time.

"I don't believe Mr. Dare is here any more," said Norman, growing tired of searching.

"Oh, yes he is," sang out Honey Bunch. She had just seen the red puppet trailer at the far end of the lot.

The children ran to the moving house and rapped on the door. Mrs. Dare opened it for them.

"Well, just see who is here!" she exclaimed. "Victor, our little friends are back again."

Mr. Dare was glad to see Norman and Honey Bunch. He invited them to come into the trailer. Honey Bunch sat down in a chair and Tommy at once made himself comfortable in her lap.

"I guess your cat missed me," she said.

"Yes, Tommy has been meowing and complaining ever since our trailer parted company with yours," declared Mr. Dare. "When did you get into camp?"

"Only a few minutes ago," said Honey

Bunch. "We spent a whole week by a waterfall."

"And we found a leather bag filled with jewelry!" broke in Norman. He forgot that he
had been warned not to tell the important
news.

"Jewelry!" exclaimed Mrs. Dare. "You
don't mean real valuable jewelry?"

"My daddy said it's worth lots of money,"
replied the little boy.

"We weren't supposed to tell about it,"
Honey Bunch reminded her playmate. But
now that Norman had told so much she decided that there was no use in trying to keep
the secret. "I found it behind the waterfall."

She described the strange place where the
pouch had been hidden.

"Why, we camped on that same site less than
a week ago!" exclaimed Mr. Dare. "We
never dreamed anything valuable was behind
the falls."

"Daddy advertised in the paper," Honey
Bunch went on. "No one ever claimed the
jewelry."

"I guess if the owner never comes it will belong to Honey Bunch and me," said Norman.

The Dares' trailer stood at the very edge of the park beside a tall hedge. Just beyond was the main highway. Unnoticed by Mr. and Mrs. Dare, a swarthy, poorly dressed man had come up close to the trailer.

Protected by the bushes, he stood listening. Honey Bunch and Norman spoke in loud tones for they were excited. Hearing the children describe the jewelry, the man crept closer.

"Well, well," he said to himself. "So that jewelry has never been claimed? Jasper, you need money, and this is your chance! It will all be very simple."

Chuckling with delight, the man stole quietly away to form a plan.

CHAPTER IX

A DARING PLAN

HONEY BUNCH and Norman did not know that anyone had overheard their words. Bidding good-bye to their friends, they ran back to report to their parents that the Dares were in camp.

"Mother, will you take Norman and me to the puppet show?" Honey Bunch pleaded. "Mr. Dare gave us free tickets."

"Why, that was very nice of him, I'm sure," returned Mrs. Morton. "How long will the show be in Fairhaven?"

The little girl had heard the man say that he and his wife expected to remain for at least a week.

"Then we'll surely see the cute marionettes perform," Mother declared. "I'll take you there in a day or two."

The following morning Honey Bunch had

just finished eating her breakfast cereal when Mr. Clark rapped on the door of the *Robin*.

"Hello," he said, "anyone up yet?"

"Oh, we've been abroad for an hour," declared Mrs. Morton, opening the door. "Do come in, Mr. Clark."

"Can't stay now," replied the man. "My own breakfast is waiting. I just wanted to show you this."

He took a newspaper from his coat pocket and spread it out on the table.

"Not bad news, I hope," said Honey Bunch's mother.

Mr. Clark didn't answer. He just pointed to an advertisement on the last page of the paper.

"What does it say, Mother?" asked Honey Bunch anxiously.

Mrs. Morton read the advertisement aloud:

"LOST: Small leather bag containing valuable jewelry. Bracelets and rings, other trinkets. Finder please notify Jasper Crone, Box 458."

"Why, that must be the bag of jewelry we

found behind the waterfall!" cried Honey
Bunch. "Will we get a big reward, Mother?"

The little girl knew that persons who lose
valuables usually offer something for their safe
return.

"The advertisement doesn't mention a reward," replied Mrs. Morton. "But of course
we're not interested in that, my dear."

"The minute I saw this ad I thought to
myself, 'We've found our man,'" declared Mr.
Clark. "The thing to do is to get in touch with
him at once."

"Yes, certainly," agreed Mrs. Morton.
"I'll show this to my husband when he comes
back from the store."

Soon Daddy Morton came trudging in with
a huge sack of groceries.

"Oh, Daddy!" cried Honey Bunch. "We've
found the man who lost the jewelry!"

Mr. Morton read the newspaper advertisement. He too thought that they had found the
person for whom they were searching.

"I'll trace this man right away," he declared. "It will be a great relief to get rid of

those valuable things. I've been afraid someone would steal the bag from our trailer."

Daddy Morton sat down and wrote a letter
to Jasper Crone. The next day he received a
note in return asking him to come to a rooming
house on Burton Street.

Mr. Morton and Mr. Clark decided to visit
the rooming house together. Honey Bunch
and Norman rode along with them in the car.

Now Jasper Crone was the same Jasper who
had overheard the children tell the Dares
about finding the jewelry. He had plotted to
get all the valuable rings and bracelets for
himself.

Daddy Morton couldn't know this, of
course, but just the same there was something
about the man which he didn't like. So he decided to be very careful.

"Will you describe the bag of jewelry which
you lost, Mr. Crone?" he asked politely.

"It was a leather bag," replied the swarthy
man.

"And the color?"

"Brown."

"Oh, no, that's not right!" cried Honey
Bunch. "The bag was black."

"I couldn't remember the color very well,"
said Jasper quickly. "But the bag is mine all
right. I hid it behind a waterfall."

Now Mr. Morton thought that the man
might have stolen the valuables. He decided
to be very cautious about turning over the
leather pouch to him.

"Do you mind telling me why you hid the
jewelry in such a strange place?" he inquired.

For a minute Jasper couldn't think of an
answer. Then he said glibly:

"My house burned down. I needed a safe
place to hide my valuables."

Daddy Morton looked quickly at Mr. Clark.
Jasper Crone's story didn't sound right at all.
If a man owned a great deal of valuable jewelry he could afford to pay a few dollars to
keep it in a bank. Certainly a waterfall wasn't
a safe place.

"Did you bring the bag of jewelry with
you?" asked the bad man eagerly.

"No, we didn't," said Daddy Morton. "So

far I'm not sure that it really belongs to you."

"How many pieces of jewelry were in the bag?" asked Mr. Clark.

"I don't just remember," muttered the man. "There were bracelets and rings."

"Will you describe one of the bracelets?" inquired Daddy Morton.

"It was gold, set with precious stones."

"Emeralds?" questioned Daddy Morton.

"Yes, that's right."

"Sorry, but it's not right," corrected Mr. Morton. "I'm afraid we can't turn over the valuables to you."

The swarthy man was very angry then, but he tried not to show it. He waited until the Morton car had driven away. When it was far down the street he jumped into his own rickety automobile and followed it. Jasper saw Honey Bunch's father return to the *Robin*.

"Probably the jewelry is hidden somewhere in that trailer," he told himself. "I'll watch my chance and maybe I'll get it."

For nearly an hour the man kept out of sight with his eyes on both the *Robin* and the *Blue-*

bird. He was pleased to see Mr. Morton
leave with his brief case in hand. Then a little later Mrs. Morton and Mrs. Clark started
away with the children.

"I wonder if our things will be perfectly
safe here," said Honey Bunch's mother anxiously. "I wish we didn't have that bag of jewelry in our trailer."

"My husband will be close by all day," answered Mrs. Clark. "He'll keep watch of
things."

Mr. Clark intended to watch the trailers
closely. However, after the two women had
taken Norman and Honey Bunch to the puppet show, he became interested in working on
his car. The recent rains had splashed it with
mud so that it needed washing.

When the task was finished, Mr. Clark discovered that the engine had a queer sound.
He worked over it for an hour, even crawling
under the car for a time.

"Now is my chance," thought Jasper, who
had been hiding near by.

He slipped from his own automobile and

stole over to the *Robin*. The door was locked but the bad man knew what to do about that. He had brought a skeleton key with him which would unlock almost any type of door.

In a moment the man was inside the Morton trailer. He opened cupboard drawers and peered into every nook and cranny. Mrs. Morton had placed the jewelry under the mattress of the couch-bed. Finally the man thought to look there.

"Ah, here it is!" he chuckled. "A rich haul, Jasper!" he told himself.

Taking the small leather pouch, he hid it under his coat. Then, waiting until Mr. Clark was out of sight, he stole back to his automobile and drove away.

A little later Mrs. Morton and Mrs. Clark returned from the puppet show with the children.

"Mother, our door is unlocked," said Honey Bunch when she tried the knob.

"How strange," murmured Mrs. Morton. "I'm certain I locked it before we went away."

"I saw you do it myself," agreed Mrs. Clark.

She called to her husband and asked him if he had been inside the Morton trailer.

"No, I've been working on the car all day," said Norman's father. "Besides, I have no key."

"Perhaps I dreamed that I locked it," remarked Mrs. Morton. "I must be more careful next time."

"Well, no harm has been done," said Mr. Clark cheerfully. "Not a soul has been around here today."

Honey Bunch opened the door and stepped into the trailer. Right away she noticed a big piece of dried mud on the clean linoleum floor. The door of a wardrobe closet was open.

"Mother!" she cried excitedly. "Someone with dirty shoes has been in our trailer!"

Honey Bunch ran her hand under the mattress of the couch. She couldn't feel the bag of jewels anywhere.

"Mother, it's gone!" she cried.

"I'm sure the leather pouch must be there," declared Mrs. Morton. "Let me see."

She felt under the mattress too but of course

the bag of jewelry could not be found. By this time Honey Bunch's mother was very worried. She pulled the mattress off on the floor, exposing the bed springs.

"The jewelry *has* been stolen!" she gasped.

Honey Bunch didn't wait to hear any more. She ran to the *Bluebird* to report the bad news to her friends. The Clarks hurried with the little girl to the *Robin*.

"I just can't believe it!" exclaimed Norman's daddy. "Why, I was here every minute of the day. How could anyone have broken into the trailer?"

"Perhaps you were so busy with your car you didn't notice," declared his wife.

"I did crawl under it for a few minutes."

"It wouldn't take very long for a man to get into the trailer," said Mrs. Clark, "especially if he had been watching for a chance."

Mrs. Morton was deeply disturbed over the loss. She said very little, though, for she did not wish Mr. Clark to think that she blamed him in the least for not having watched more closely.

"How did anyone suspect that we had the jewelry hidden in the trailer?" she murmured. "Honey Bunch, were you careful not to speak of it to anyone?"

The little girl shifted uneasily from one foot to the other. She didn't like to tell on Norman. The boy started edging toward the door, but his father grasped his little son by the arm so he could not wriggle away.

"Just a minute, young man!" he said sternly.

"Oh, it wasn't my fault the jewelry was stolen," said Norman. "I didn't tell anyone about it except Mr. and Mrs. Dare."

"I feel certain they are trustworthy people," remarked Mrs. Morton.

"True," agreed Mr. Clark, "but some other person might have overheard the conversation."

"Norman did talk in a loud voice," said Honey Bunch. "And I did, too."

"I blame myself more than anyone else," declared Mr. Clark. "I should have guarded the trailer better."

The grown-ups searched the *Robin* carefully for clues. They found no trace of the person who had taken the jewels. Norman's father went to report the loss to the manager of the tourist park.

Honey Bunch and Norman wished that they could do something to help. They went about the lot asking campers if they had seen anyone trying to break into the Morton trailer.

"I guess no one saw that old thief at all," sighed Norman in disappointment.

Lady Clare followed the children about the park. Now, for no reason at all, she wriggled through a hole in the hedge and started toward the main road.

"There goes your cat, Honey Bunch," called Norman. "You better get her 'fore she's struck by a car." The little boy felt too tired to go after the animal himself.

"Lady Clare! Lady Clare!" coaxed Honey Bunch anxiously. "Come back here!"

When the cat did not obey, she scrambled through the tall hedge after her pet. Cars were whizzing past on the main road.

"Lady Clare!" called Honey Bunch again.

She never had been able to train the cat to be careful in traffic.

Lady Clare turned her head very slowly. She had a bored look as she waited for the little girl to pick her up.

"You bad, bad kitty," scolded Honey Bunch. "Don't you know you might have been run over?"

She started to carry her pet back to the tourist park. Bending down to crawl through a gap in the hedge, the little girl noticed a large puddle of oil on the ground. An automobile must have been parked in the tall grass for a long time. The grass was trampled, too.

Then Honey Bunch saw something else. A black and white metal object was lying almost at her feet. She knew at once that it was an important discovery.

"Norman!" she called. "Come here quick and see what I've found!"

CHAPTER X

A BOAT RIDE

NORMAN forgot that he was tired and ran over to the gap in the hedge.

"What have you found, Honey Bunch?" he cried.

The little girl held up the shiny piece of metal which she had discovered in the tall grass.

"Why, that's only a license plate from an automobile!" scoffed Norman. "I thought you had something important, Honey Bunch."

"I guess I know it's a license plate," returned Honey Bunch, a little hurt. "But it could be a clue."

"A clue to what?"

"Why, to the person who ran off with the jewelry. Maybe he parked his car right here by that hole in the hedge. I'm going to show it to Mother."

Honey Bunch ran back to the *Robin,* carrying Lady Clare under one arm and the license plate under the other.

At first Mrs. Morton did not think the clue was of much importance. But when she heard where the automobile had been parked, she called Mr. and Mrs. Clark. They all went together to inspect the ground near the hedge.

"It's evident a car stood here for a length of time," declared Mr. Clark. "From this gap in the hedge one gets a clear view of the *Robin.*"

"Would it be possible to trace the license number?" asked Mrs. Morton.

"Yes, all numbers are registered. I'll take care of the matter right away."

Without wasting another minute, Mr. Clark started downtown to see if he could check up on the owner of the car.

At five o'clock Daddy Morton came back from his business appointment. Honey Bunch met him at the park gate and told him what had happened. At first her father thought she was joking.

"Oh, Daddy, someone really did steal the

jewelry," the little girl insisted. "Every speck of it is gone."

Just then Mr. Clark came down the road, walking very fast. Daddy Morton waited for him, and the two men talked together.

"Honey Bunch tells me the jewelry has been stolen! I can't believe it."

"It's true all right," said Mr. Clark soberly. "Your little girl picked up the license plate of an automobile which had been parked near the hedge. I've been tracing the number."

"Any luck?"

Mr. Clark nodded. "Yes, but I'm afraid we'll never see that jewelry again. The license number had been made out to Jasper Crone."

Honey Bunch opened her eyes very wide at this bit of information. She remembered that he was the same man who had claimed all the jewels belonged to him.

"The scamp!" exclaimed Daddy Morton. "When he couldn't get us to give him the jewels he decided to take them by force."

Mr. Morton and Mr. Clark both made up their minds that Jasper had stolen the leather bag. They were certain of it a little later when a man whose trailer stood near the Dares' came to make an interesting report. He told Mr. Morton he had seen a dark-skinned man crouching close to the fence one day.

"The fellow was listening to what was being said inside the Dare trailer. Just after he went away I saw the children come out."

"Probably the man Jasper heard them tell Mr. and Mrs. Dare about the jewels," Mr. Morton said. "That was how he learned the bag had been hidden back of the waterfall."

Norman was sorry he had given away the secret. He promised to be very careful in the future. And Honey Bunch was sorry she had added to his story.

"It's no use locking the barn door after the horse has been stolen," sighed the little girl, using Mrs. Miller's words. The laundress always used that expression when it was too late to be cautious.

"The trailer *was* locked," declared Norman, "so I guess it wasn't all my fault."

Daddy Morton went at once to the police to

report the loss. He asked the officers to be on the lookout for Jasper Crone.

The story was printed in all the local newspapers. A photographer came and took a picture of the *Robin*. He had Honey Bunch sit on the steps, so her picture was in one of the papers too.

Now Jasper Crone, after taking the bag of jewels, had driven far out into the country. He parked his car along a river where no one would see it.

"This will be a good place to stay," he thought. "I'll keep away from the city for a few weeks. By that time the Morton trailer will have moved to another town."

After a few days the police told Mr. Morton they were afraid they might never be able to trace the thief. The man had vanished completely. Norman felt worse than ever about the missing jewelry.

Once more the little fellow resolved he would do something especially nice in order to make up for the trouble he had caused. As Honey Bunch well knew, Norman's memory was none too good. He just couldn't help being an active boy, and forgetting many things he should do.

The children often walked along the shore of the lake to look at the pretty boats. They saw several canoes and sailboats as well as a few large yachts.

Norman admired especially a fine speed boat owned by a Mr. and Mrs. Farret. The couple had a little baby named June. One day Honey Bunch saw the child toddling toward the water's edge. She ran and brought June back to her mother. After that her parents became very friendly with the Mortons and the Clarks.

"I wish the Farrets would give us a ride in their boat," said Norman more than once to his playmate.

One day when the children were out on the pier, the man smiled at them in a very friendly way.

"My wife and I are going for a little spin," he called. "Would you like to come along?"

Would they? Norman was so excited that

he nearly tumbled off the dock into the water.

"Do you think we should go, Norman?" whispered Honey Bunch. "Mother may wonder where we are."

"Oh, we'll be right back," said Norman. He was impatient to get on the boat. "Come along, Honey Bunch."

"Your parents won't care, I suppose," remarked Mr. Farret, helping the children into the nice leather seats.

"Oh, no!" said Norman quickly before Honey Bunch could say a word.

Mrs. Farret stepped into the boat with Baby June. Then the engine was started. It made such a roar Honey Bunch couldn't hear what anyone said to her.

"Hold tight!" shouted Mr. Farret.

He pulled a lever and the speed boat moved away from the pier. It traveled swiftly down the lake, bumping over the little wavelets.

"Oh, this is fun!" cried Honey Bunch, laughing right out loud.

"Make it go faster!" shouted Norman.

The boat rounded a bend and swept past a

tiny green island. A bathing beach was left
behind and they overtook several canoes.
Finally they sped into a large river.

"We must be going at least a hundred miles
an hour!" cried Norman.

Honey Bunch and Norman were having a
thrilling experience. They never once stopped to think that they were traveling a long
distance from Fairhaven. As for Mr. and
Mrs. Farret, they believed that the children's
parents did not expect them at the trailers for
some time.

After the boat had sped many miles down
the stream, Honey Bunch and Norman noticed
that they were drawing near a town.

"Yonder is Elmwood," said Mr. Farret,
pointing toward the cluster of buildings. "A
quaint little river town. We might stop there
for ice cream."

"Perhaps the children are in a hurry to get
back," suggested Mrs. Farret.

"Oh, no!" spoke up Norman quickly.
"We're not in a hurry at all."

"Then we'll have our ice cream and cake,"

laughed Mr. Farret. "The sun is still high. We'll be back in Fairhaven long before supper time."

The boat soon drew up at a pier. Mr. Farret helped everyone out and led the way to a nice store where music was being played. They sat down in a room away from the counter and near a window. Honey Bunch ordered a strawberry soda.

"What would you like, Norman?" inquired Mr. Farret.

The little boy pretended to study the menu although he couldn't read it very well.

"I'll take a big chocolate sundae with nuts, bananas and red cherries," he said at last.

"Aren't you afraid you'll get sick, eating so much sweet stuff?" smiled Mrs. Farret. "I fear your mother wouldn't exactly approve of it." She asked the waiter to bring Norman a plain chocolate sundae instead.

Honey Bunch sat beside the plate glass window. While she sipped her soda through two straws she watched the people walking up and down the street.

Suddenly the little girl straightened in her chair. An old rattle-trap auto was driving up to the curb. One of its license plates was missing!

A dark-skinned man stepped down from the running board. He had his cap pulled low over his eyes. Honey Bunch caught her breath sharply for she recognized Jasper Crone.

CHAPTER XI

ICE CREAM FOR TWO

WHEN Honey Bunch saw that the man really was Jasper, she tried to attract Norman's attention by giving him a little kick with her foot.

"Quit kicking—" Norman began, and then stopped short.

He noticed the queer way Honey Bunch was acting. She was trying to make him look out of the window.

"That man's Jasper," Honey Bunch whispered in his ear.

The children saw the fellow leave his car and enter the ice cream shop. Instead of coming into the room where they were he stepped into a telephone booth.

Honey Bunch knew that she just had to do something right away. She didn't want the

man to get away, because then they never
would recover the stolen jewels.

The little girl was so excited over seeing
Jasper Crone that she didn't take time to explain anything to Mr. and Mrs. Farret. She
simply pushed back her chair and ran right
out of the room. Norman couldn't bear to be
left behind, so he jumped up and followed his
playmate.

"What shall we do, Honey Bunch?" he
asked anxiously.

"Let's look in the car while that man is gone.
Maybe he hid the jewels somewhere inside his
auto."

The children darted outdoors to the run-
down old machine standing by the curb a little way down the street. Honey Bunch looked
in the glove compartment and on the floor,
but she could not find the stolen jewels anywhere. Then she noticed an old sweater which
had been jammed down into the corner of the
seat. As she jerked it away, she cried out:

"I've found the jewels, Norman! The bag
is here!"

"Hurry, Honey Bunch!" warned Norman, who was watching. "He's coming!"

Through the plate glass window he had seen Jasper leave the telephone booth. He would return to his car!

Honey Bunch jumped down from the running board with the leather pouch in her hand. The little girl was badly frightened. She looked up and down the street, but there seemed no place where she might hide.

"Drop it and run!" advised Norman. He turned and bolted back into the doorway of a shop building.

Honey Bunch didn't wish to lose the jewels, yet she was afraid to take them with her. Quick as a flash she tossed the leather bag on the street under the car. Then she darted away to hide behind another parked automobile.

Jasper Crone came out of the ice cream shop and looked about him. He did not see either of the children, so climbing into his car he drove away, leaving the bag of jewels lying in plain view on the street.

"Pick it up quick, Honey Bunch!" called

Norman anxiously. "Before he comes back!"

The little girl moved from behind the parked car where she had been hiding. Cautiously she picked up the leather bag. She knew by its heavy feel that the jewels were still in it.

"What shall I do with it, Norman?" she asked. She was afraid that Jasper might discover his loss and come back looking for the leather bag.

"Maybe I can put it under my coat," said the little boy.

"Oh, the bag is too large for that."

Honey Bunch couldn't think of a single place to hide the jewels. Then she looked across the street and noticed a grocery store.

"I have an idea!" she cried. "Hold this a minute, Norman."

She handed the boy the bag and ran across the street. Norman couldn't imagine what the little girl intended to do as he saw her go into the grocery store.

Honey Bunch walked right up to the counter where a man in a white apron was waiting on a lady. After a while the woman went away and the grocer smiled down at his young customer.

"What would you like today?" he asked. "An all-day sucker?"

Honey Bunch shook her head. "Please, I'd like a great big paper bag."

"One with a hole in it?" teased the man.

"Oh, no! A nice new bag."

"So that you can blow it up and make it go bang!" laughed the grocer. He reached under the counter for a paper sack. "How will this one do?"

"That one is just right," declared Honey Bunch.

"You'll need a bellows to blow it up," laughed the man. "But it should make a good loud bang when you crack it open."

Honey Bunch thanked the groceryman. She didn't tell him her real reason for wanting the sack. Hurrying across the street, she found Norman waiting behind a parked car.

"It took you an awful long time, Honey Bunch," he complained.

"I hurried as fast as I could, Norman. And look what I have! We can drop the jewels into this paper sack! Then no one will guess what we're carrying."

The children placed the pouch of jewels inside the larger sack.

"Let me carry it," said Norman.

"All right," agreed Honey Bunch, "but we must go back to the ice cream store now. Mrs. Farret will be looking for us if we stay out here any longer."

The Farrets had been a little surprised because the children had acted so strangely. Mrs. Farret told her husband she thought he should go after Norman and Honey Bunch.

"Oh, they're all right," replied her husband. "I can see Honey Bunch from here. She's running over to the grocery store."

"I wonder what strange notion got into the child's mind," Mrs. Farret mused.

In a minute or two Norman and Honey Bunch returned to the ice cream shop carrying the paper sack. They slid back into their chairs.

"Well, well, what have you youngsters in that big bag?" laughed Mr. Farret. "I know it's something you bought at the grocery store."

The children didn't say a word. They had agreed they wouldn't tell anyone about finding the jewels. The last time they had talked about it Jasper had overheard them and made trouble.

"You act very mysterious," smiled Mrs. Farret.

"This is a secret package," Honey Bunch explained. "We can't tell anyone what is in it."

"I'll venture I could guess," chuckled Mr. Farret. "Oranges!"

Honey Bunch shook her head. "Not oranges," she said, "but please don't guess any more."

Mrs. Farret smiled across the table at the little girl. She understood that the children wished to keep their secret all to themselves, so she said to her husband:

"I think we should be starting back to Fairhaven now. Baby June is getting tired. We shouldn't keep her away from home any longer."

"Yes," agreed Mr. Farret, "we'll return at once."

He paid the bill and they all left the ice cream store together. Suddenly Norman gave a little cry of alarm. He stopped dead still in the street.

"What's wrong now, young man?" asked Mr. Farret.

"I—I stubbed my toe," stammered Norman, looking down.

It was true he had stumbled, but that wasn't all that was the matter. The little boy had seen a car coming down the street. It was a rickety vehicle with a missing license plate.

"O-ooh, Honey Bunch," he whispered, "what shall we do?"

His playmate tried to act as if she wasn't at all frightened. She hoped Jasper Crone would drive straight past and not see them.

Cars were parked in front of the ice cream shop, so the man drew up just across the street by the grocery store. Norman and Honey

Bunch could tell by his actions that the driver was very angry indeed.

"I've been robbed!" he shouted. "Robbed! Someone stole a valuable bag from my car!"

Honey Bunch and Norman didn't wait to hear any more. They started to walk away as fast as they could.

"Let's hurry to the boat," Honey Bunch urged Mr. and Mrs. Farret. She clutched the paper sack tightly in her small fist. "I think maybe Mother and Daddy need me back right away."

CHAPTER XII

FIRE!

MR. AND MRS. FARRET could not walk very fast because they took turns carrying Baby June. They did not understand why Norman and Honey Bunch had taken a notion all of a sudden to return to the boat.

"We'll run on ahead," called Norman over his shoulder.

He took Honey Bunch's hand and they scampered down the street. Never once did they look back until they reached the pier.

"Is he after us?" gasped Honey Bunch, out of breath.

"No, he's not coming yet," replied Norman. "But I wish Mr. and Mrs. Farret wouldn't take so long getting here."

In a few minutes the couple reached the dock. Baby June was crying.

"Poor little thing, she's so tired," said Mrs.

Farret. "We shouldn't have kept her out this long."

Both she and her husband were occupied trying to quiet the baby. They didn't think to ask Norman and Honey Bunch why they were acting so strangely.

Mr. Farret hustled the children into the speed boat and started the engine. Their young guests heaved sighs of relief as shore was left behind. They were now safe from Jasper Crone!

Honey Bunch felt a little tired after such an exciting day and was glad they were going back to the trailer. Soon the Fairhaven pier loomed up before them.

"Why, there's Daddy standing on the dock!" exclaimed the child. "And Mother, too!"

Norman's parents were waiting on the pier also. Mr. and Mrs. Farret understood then that something was wrong.

"John," she said anxiously to her husband. "You surely told the Mortons and the Clarks we were taking the children for a ride, didn't you?"

"Why no, I thought you spoke to Mrs. Morton about it this morning."

"I meant to do it, but I didn't see her," replied Mrs. Farret. "Oh, dear, I'm afraid they have worried over the children."

The boat drew up at the pier. Honey Bunch and Norman didn't say a word as they stepped out. They knew they deserved a scolding.

"Honey Bunch, we've been very worried about you," said her father. "Why did you go away without telling us?"

"No doubt this young man can give us the reason," said Mr. Clark, looking at Norman.

"I feel that we are the ones to blame," spoke up Mrs. Farret. "You see, I thought you knew the children were with us. I can't tell you how sorry I am."

"As a matter of fact, we were only worried for a very short time," replied Honey Bunch's mother. "A dock hand told us he had seen the children ride away in your boat."

After the Farrets explained how the mixup had occurred, Honey Bunch and Norman were taken back to the trailers. The grown-ups did not give them a chance to say a word about the bag of jewels.

"Mother," began Honey Bunch, "when we were in the ice cream store—"

"Oh, dear, did you have ice cream?" sighed Mrs. Morton. "Now I suppose you'll want no supper."

"Yes, I will," said Honey Bunch quickly. "Mother, when we were in the ice cream store—"

"I'm sure you didn't realize you were doing wrong," went on her mother, "but you shouldn't have gone away as you did. Haven't we talked about it many times?"

"Yes," agreed Honey Bunch, hanging her head. "I didn't stop to think."

Mrs. Morton did not like to punish the little girl. She felt that if it hadn't been for Norman, her daughter would have taken time to ask if she might ride in the boat.

"Honey Bunch," she told her little girl, "I must send you to bed as soon as you have had your supper."

"Mother—" began the little girl again.

"Now don't protest, dear. You really are getting off lightly. You caused us all a great deal of worry."

Honey Bunch hadn't intended to say a word about being sent to bed. She had meant to tell her mother about finding the jewels. Why did grown-ups sometimes refuse to listen?

Mrs. Morton prepared Honey Bunch's supper right away. After the little girl had eaten she was tucked under the cot covers. She didn't mind this because she knew that Norman had been sent to bed too. Yet she didn't like to go to sleep without telling her mother about the bag of jewels.

Mrs. Morton picked up her small daughter's blue frock and neatly folded it. As she reached down to put a pair of scuffed sandals away, she noticed the paper sack which Honey Bunch had carried.

"Why, what is this?" she questioned.

"Oh," sighed Honey Bunch, "I've been trying to tell you but you wouldn't listen."

Mrs. Morton picked up the heavy bag.

"I'm very sorry, Honey Bunch," she said. "I didn't realize you were trying to tell me anything. What is in the sack?"

"Jewels!" cried Honey Bunch.

"Jewels? Not the rings and bracelets we lost?"

"Look and see!" exclaimed Honey Bunch gaily.

Mrs. Morton opened the big paper bag and took out the leather pouch. Inside were the lost bracelets and rings. Not a single piece of jewelry was missing.

"Honey Bunch, where did you find this?" gasped Mrs. Morton.

Without waiting for the little girl to reply she called the little girl's daddy who was outside the trailer. Mr. Morton was amazed when he saw the jewels.

"I never expected to get them back!" he exclaimed. "Honey Bunch, you are a marvel! Where did you find this bag?"

"In Jasper's old car," returned Honey Bunch. "Under a sweater."

"The police have searched everywhere for

that man!" declared Mr. Morton, laughing a bit. "And here our Honey Bunch locates him with no trouble at all."

"Where did you see the car, dear?" asked her mother.

"Just outside an ice cream store. The car drove up to the curb. That bad man got out and came into the place to telephone."

Honey Bunch told just how she and Norman had found the bag of jewels. Mr. Morton declared the children were very clever to think of placing the leather pouch in the grocery sack. Of course, such high praise made Honey Bunch feel very proud indeed.

"Daddy," she asked unexpectedly, "do I have to stay in bed now?"

"We—ll," Mr. Morton said and looked at his wife. Then they both laughed.

The little girl hoped they would tell her she could get up. Instead, her mother said, "It's very near your regular bedtime now anyway. And you're tired. So you might as well turn over and go to sleep."

Norman had told his parents about finding

the jewels. In the morning the Clarks came over to the *Robin* to look at the valuables. Honey Bunch heard Mrs. Clark tell her mother it was a lucky thing the children had gone on the boat with the Farrets, for otherwise the stolen jewels might never have been recovered.

"That leather bag turned up at just the right moment," declared Mr. Morton. "Another day and we shouldn't have been here."

Honey Bunch glanced up quickly from a picture book she was looking at.

"Daddy, are we going back home?" she asked.

"Yes, dear, my business here is finished. But we'll take a long while for the return trip."

Honey Bunch and Norman were sorry to leave Fairhaven. They disliked saying good-bye to the Farrets and Mr. and Mrs. Dare.

"We'll be sorry to see you go too," declared the puppet show lady when she heard that the two trailers were starting back to Barham.

"When will you leave?" asked Mr. Dare.

"In the morning when dawn cracks," replied Honey Bunch.

"She means at 'crack of dawn,'" explained Norman, who had heard Mrs. Miller use that same expression. "We're stopping a day at the waterfall."

"You don't expect to find another bag of jewels there, do you?" chuckled Mr. Dare.

"Oh, no," said Honey Bunch, "but we're going to look for the person who hid the rings and bracelets behind the waterfall."

"You and Norman are very fortunate at finding things," smiled Mr. Dare. "It wouldn't surprise me if you should locate the owner of those jewels."

Right then and there Honey Bunch and Norman decided they would try very hard to find the person who had lost the valuables. If they could only trace the old hermit they thought he might be able to help them in their search.

Honey Bunch told Mr. and Mrs. Dare she wished that they would bring their puppet show to Barham. Norman said he did too.

"We'll probably get back there again next summer," replied Mr. Dare. "We hope so anyway."

In saying good-bye, he gave each of the children a puppet. Norman received a funny little colored boy doll while Honey Bunch was presented with a chubby, jolly looking Mammy doll.

"Now we can have a puppet show of our own, Honey Bunch!" cried Norman. "These dolls are lots better than whisk brooms."

The children thanked the Dares and hurried away to show the presents to their parents.

"Mother, I wish I could give that nice lady a gift," said Honey Bunch.

"That would be kind, dear," returned her mother. "Let's see what we have."

She looked in the drawer of the wardrobe closet. There she found a fine lace handkerchief which had never been used.

"Do you think Mrs. Dare would like this?" asked Mrs. Morton.

Honey Bunch felt certain that the puppet show lady would. She and her mother

wrapped the lace handkerchief in tissue paper
and ribbons. Then the little girl carried the
gift over to the *Bluebird*.

"It was sweet of you to bring this to me,"
said Mrs. Dare. Tears came into her eyes.
"I'll think of you, Honey Bunch, every time I
use it."

That night everyone went to bed early. By
six o'clock the next morning both the *Bluebird*
and the *Robin* would be swinging along the
road.

Honey Bunch felt a little sad as she snuggled
down under the blankets. This would be her
very last night in Fairhaven!

In a short while the little girl was fast asleep.
Usually she didn't wake up until morning.
But toward midnight something aroused her.

At first she thought that her mother had
spoken to her. But Mrs. Morton was still
asleep. Just then a bell clanged outside the
trailer. That was the sound which had disturbed the little girl.

Honey Bunch jumped out of bed and ran
over to the window. She saw a fire engine

drive down the road between the narrow lane of parked trailers!

"Mother! Daddy!" shouted the little girl. "Something is burning up!"

Mr. and Mrs. Morton were awake even before the little girl called them. They hurried to the window also.

The fire engine had stopped far down the road near the fence. Flames could be seen shooting high up into the dark sky.

"That fire is down by the Dares' trailer," said Mr. Morton anxiously. "I hope they're in no danger."

"Oh, Mother—" wailed Honey Bunch.

At that moment someone pounded on the door of the *Robin*.

"Are you awake, folks?" called Mr. Clark. "The Dare trailer is on fire!"

CHAPTER XIII

LOST PUPPETS

BEFORE anyone could open the door, Mr. Clark hurried away to help put out the flames.

"Oh, how dreadful!" gasped Mrs. Morton.

"I'll get down there as quickly as I can," declared her husband. He began pulling on his shoes.

"Mother, will the trailer burn up?" Honey Bunch asked anxiously.

"Perhaps they can save it, dear, but I'm afraid not. The fire seems to have such a head start. The wind will make it worse, too."

Mrs. Morton dressed as fast as she could and helped Honey Bunch with her clothes. As they ran out of the trailer they met Norman and Mrs. Clark going to the fire too.

"Such a pity!" murmured Norman's mother. "I doubt that anything will be saved. I was awake when the fire started. The trailer seemed to burst into flames everywhere at once."

"Mr. and Mrs. Dare—"

"They escaped with just the clothes on their backs," replied Mrs. Clark. "I saw Mr. Dare run to sound the alarm."

"Will all the nice puppets be burned?" asked Honey Bunch. "And Tommy?"

"Surely they got the cat out," said Mrs. Clark.

Honey Bunch and Norman didn't think she sounded any too confident. They were terribly worried.

A little sob came into Honey Bunch's throat as she thought of Tommy. They simply *must* save the beautiful cat!

When they drew near the blazing trailer, Norman broke away from his mother. He thought the thing for him to do would be to rush right into the burning vehicle and rescue Tommy and the puppets.

"Norman!" called his mother frantically. "Come back!"

The little boy did not hear her. He was in

such a hurry to try to save things that he didn't look where he was going.

A length of hose lay in his path. He stumbled over it and down he sprawled in a puddle of water. A fireman picked Norman up and set him on his feet.

"Get back to your mother," he warned the lad sternly. "This is no place for you."

"But I want to save Tommy," wailed Norman. "The cat will burn to death."

"The cat is safe enough," said the fireman gruffly. "But you're a pest here."

Mrs. Clark came hurrying up and caught her little son by the hand. She held tightly to him after that.

The firemen were doing the best they could to put out the blaze, but there was no chance of saving the pretty red trailer. It would burn to the ground.

Honey Bunch saw Mrs. Dare leaning against a tree near by. She was holding Tommy in her arms. Tears were streaming down her cheeks.

Mrs. Morton took Honey Bunch by the

hand and went over to talk with the woman.

"We've lost everything except our car and Tommy," said Mrs. Dare sadly. "Even the puppets burned."

"Don't cry, please," Honey Bunch said comfortingly. "Mrs. Miller always says nothing's so bad it couldn't be worse."

"That's true," agreed the woman, trying to smile. "I suppose it's lucky we weren't burned to death in our beds."

"How did the fire start?" inquired Mrs. Morton.

"I don't know. When we woke up the entire trailer was ablaze. We barely escaped with Tommy."

"Possibly it started from a gasoline stove," suggested Mrs. Morton.

Mrs. Dare shook her head. "There was no explosion, I'm sure of that."

"Do you think the fire could have been caused by someone dropping a lighted match just outside?"

"It doesn't seem possible. The fire blazed up too quickly for that."

Honey Bunch had her own idea regarding the cause of the fire.

"Maybe Jasper Crone did it!" she whispered to Norman. "He'd be just mean enough to start such a thing."

"Yes, he would," agreed the lad. "I'll bet he was angry because he lost the bag of jewels."

The Mortons asked Mr. and Mrs. Dare to spend the remainder of the night in their trailer.

"You are very kind," returned the woman, "but we have promised to stay with other friends. Everyone has been so wonderful to us in our misfortune."

"Have you made any plans about the future?" inquired Daddy Morton.

"Not yet," said Mr. Dare. "This fire has been heart-breaking. But we'll start up again with a better puppet show."

"If I may lend you any money—"

"No, we have some saved up. We'll get along all right, thank you."

Honey Bunch and Norman whispered together for a moment. Then they told Mr. and

Mrs. Dare they would like to give back the puppets they had received as gifts.

"No, you keep them," the woman said, deeply touched. "We shall have to make up an entirely new set anyway."

The fire had died down, so the Mortons took Honey Bunch back to the *Robin*. As the little girl was tumbling drowsily into bed she heard her father remark:

"Queer thing about that fire. I'd like to know how it started."

"Daddy, I think I know!" exclaimed Honey Bunch.

"I don't believe you do," replied her father in a strange voice.

"Yes, I do," insisted Honey Bunch earnestly. "Jasper Crone started it on purpose."

"Jasper Crone!" Daddy Morton repeated slowly. "No one could prove such a thing. Honey Bunch, you must never tell anyone what you think about it."

"It is not right to accuse a person unless you have absolute proof, dear," added her mother.

Before Honey Bunch fell asleep she made

up her mind that she would try to find the "absolute proof" one must have before making an accusation. Norman would help her get it.

"Only it won't be a bit easy," the little girl thought, " 'cause tomorrow we'll be on our way home."

Before Honey Bunch could realize it, her eyes opened wide and it was time for her to get up and dress. The *Bluebird* pulled out of camp first.

"We beat you!" Norman shouted as he waved at Honey Bunch.

The *Robin* soon took to the road. Mr. Morton drove fast enough to catch up with the other trailer.

"Mother, what will Mr. and Mrs. Dare do now that they have no place in which to live?" Honey Bunch asked thoughtfully.

"They will stay with friends for a while," replied Mrs. Morton. "Then I suppose they will buy a new trailer."

The day wore on. Honey Bunch and Norman grew tired of riding such a long time, but the two trailers did not halt until they reached the camp by the waterfall. By that time it was evening, so the children could not go out to play until the next morning. Right after breakfast they put on their sun suits and ran out in the sunshine.

"Let's hunt for more jewels!" cried Honey Bunch.

"Oh, there won't be any others hidden around here," scoffed Norman.

He picked up a handful of round stones, and one by one made them skip across the water.

"There *might* be another bag of jewels, or maybe pieces of gold behind the falls," declared Honey Bunch. "I'm going to look."

Her playmate paid no attention as the little girl squeezed her body flat against the rocky ledge. Very cautiously she edged behind the great stream of water.

"O-oh! I'm getting all splashed!" she shouted. "It's cold!"

"You won't find any more jewels, Honey Bunch," her companion called out.

Scarcely were Norman's words spoken when

the little girl gave a scream. For just a second the boy thought she had fallen into the river.

"I've found something! I've found something!" called Honey Bunch in an excited voice.

Norman dropped all his stones and raced to the waterfall.

"Another bag of jewels?" he shouted in great excitement.

He could see that Honey Bunch was holding something in her hand but he couldn't tell just what it was. The little girl didn't answer him. She backed out into the light with her find. Her sun suit was dripping wet.

"Why, it's only an old hat!" exclaimed Norman in disappointment. "A man's hat. I thought you had found a treasure, Honey Bunch."

At that moment Mrs. Morton appeared in the doorway of the *Robin*. Honey Bunch ran to show her the man's hat.

"Where did you find this, dear?" asked Mrs. Morton.

"Behind the waterfall," said Honey Bunch. "It was in plain sight. Only I got wet when I reached to pick it up."

"It's nothing but an old hat," said Norman again.

"On the contrary," declared Mrs. Morton, "it may be an important clue."

Norman's eyes opened wide at that announcement. He was sorry he hadn't been the one to find the hat.

"Maybe it was dropped by the man who hid the bag of jewels!" cried Honey Bunch.

"I had the same thought in mind, dear. Are you quite sure it was not behind the falls when we camped here before?"

"Oh, no," said the little girl, "it wasn't there until today. Don't you remember, Mother? Daddy reached way in himself."

"Yes, you are right, dear. He surely would have noticed the hat if it had been there. This clue has been left recently."

"Mother, do you suppose the man who lost the jewels left the hat?"

"I should imagine so, Honey Bunch. Perhaps he came back to search for the leather bag and his hat fell off back there."

Mrs. Morton examined the hat carefully. Inside the soiled band she noticed the imprint of the initials "L.T." and the words "Plaza City."

"Maybe Jasper lost the hat," said Norman importantly.

Mrs. Morton shook her head. "I doubt it, Norman. You see, 'L.T.' couldn't stand for the name Jasper Crone."

She showed the hat to Daddy Morton and to Mr. and Mrs. Clark. They all agreed that it was an important clue. However, no one had ever heard of a man living in Plaza City whose initials were "L.T." For that matter, they knew no one at all in that city.

Norman and Honey Bunch hoped that the man would return again to the waterfall. They decided to keep close watch so that they would not miss him. Hours at a time they spent playing near the brook.

"Maybe he sees us here and is afraid to

come," said Honey Bunch after they had
waited a long while.

"Let's hide somewhere," suggested Norman.
"Then he might show himself."

"There's no place to hide," said his playmate. The banks of the stream at this point
were quite bare of bushes.

"We could build a little stone house!" cried
Norman.

"Wouldn't that be a lot of work?"

"No, it would be easy!" laughed Norman,
who liked to build things. "I know just how to
do it."

The little boy selected a level place not far
from the waterfall.

"First we'll need a great big pile of rocks,"
he declared.

The children ran up and down the stream,
searching for smooth, round stones. Soon they
had a large pile. Then Norman built up the
walls. He couldn't make them very high because they kept falling down.

"We need a roof," he said. "Honey Bunch,
see if you can find some boards."

"I know where I can get them!" cried the little girl.

Farther downstream a log had fallen across the brook. Sticks and boards had caught against it, making a dam.

Honey Bunch chose some of the larger boards and carried them back to Norman. He laid them across the stone walls for a roof.

"There, it's all finished," he declared proudly after a while.

"I'm awfully tired," sighed Honey Bunch. She had carried considerably more stones than Norman had.

"This will make a dandy hide-out!" said the little boy. "Only we ought to cover it with brush. See if you can find some brush, Honey Bunch."

"I don't know where there is any."

"I'll get some in the woods," declared Norman.

He ran off and soon came back dragging the dead branch of a tree.

"How will we get into the house?" asked Honey Bunch. "There's no door or window."

"That's easy," laughed Norman. "We'll go through the roof."

After covering the house with brush, he took off one of the boards. The children climbed down inside. Then Norman fitted the roof board back into place.

"It's dark in here," said Honey Bunch. "I can't see a thing."

"All hide-outs are dark," declared the little boy.

In a few minutes it was much easier to see. Light filtered in through the chinks between the rocks. The children were able to peep out and keep close watch of the waterfall.

"I wish that man would hurry up and come," sighed Honey Bunch.

It was very tiring to sit in such cramped quarters. Her feet felt all prickly and numb.

Norman grew weary of waiting too. He squirmed about until he dislodged one of the stones.

"Be careful!" warned Honey Bunch. "You're breaking down our hide-out."

"I don't care if I am," said the little boy

crossly. He stood up quickly and cracked his head hard against the roof.

"Oh, did you hurt yourself?" asked Honey Bunch, who was a very sympathetic child.

" 'Course I did," said Norman, feeling the bump on his head. "This old roof is a bother anyway."

He lifted off the boards and threw them to the ground. Honey Bunch liked the stone house much better that way. It was lighter, and they could see the clear blue sky.

All that day the children kept close watch of the waterfall. No one appeared. The next day was exactly the same. Even Honey Bunch began to grow discouraged. Daddy Morton spoke of starting for home. The little girl feared they never would find the owner of the jewels.

The third day Norman didn't even wish to keep watch. He thought that it would only be a waste of time.

"Please, Norman," coaxed Honey Bunch. "Things always happen when you least expect them to. That's what Mrs. Miller says."

"Oh, all right," Norman gave in.

The morning wore on slowly. It was very warm in the little stone house.

"I'm not going to stay here any longer," announced the little boy finally. "I'd rather wade in the brook."

"Oh, Norman—" Honey Bunch gripped his arm. "Look up there!"

She pointed overhead. A large bird was flying toward the waterfall.

"Say, that one is a whopper!" exclaimed Norman in awe. "Maybe it's an eagle."

"The bird has something in its beak," Honey Bunch whispered excitedly. "Can you see what it is?"

Norman shaded his eyes from the sun. The bird was flying closer, but he couldn't tell what it was carrying.

"It's circling over the waterfall, Honey Bunch!"

"Keep down out of sight," warned the little girl.

The children crouched low in their hide-out. Watching through a gap in the stones,

they saw the huge bird alight not far away.
His wings were large and strong looking.

"Norman, look!" whispered Honey Bunch.

The bird had disappeared in the gap behind
the falls.

"Did you see that?" gasped Honey Bunch.
"The bird carried something in there."

Before the children could move, the eagle
again came into view. Its beak now was
empty. While Norman and Honey Bunch
watched in surprise, it flew away.

"The bird hid something behind the waterfall!" cried Norman. "Let's find out what
it is!"

In his haste to get out of the stone house, the
little boy dislodged several rocks. Down tumbled one of the walls. Norman didn't even
notice this, so eager was he to get out.

"Be careful!" called Honey Bunch. "The
rocks are slippery."

Norman paid no attention. For that matter,
he did not hear the warning. He was too
intent upon being the first one to see what had
been hidden by the big bird.

Suddenly Norman slipped just as his playmate had feared he might do.   He tried hard
to regain his balance.

"Help!" he shouted.

Honey Bunch tried to reach her little friend
but she couldn't move quickly enough.   With
a big splash the boy fell into a deep part of
the river.

CHAPTER XIV

NORMAN'S RESCUE

THE little boy tried to stand up in the water. His feet didn't touch bottom at all. He had fallen into a deep hole!

When Norman attempted to cry for help, not a word came from his throat—just a choking, gurgling sound. His head went down under the water. Honey Bunch had never been so frightened before in all her life.

"Help! Help!" she screamed. "Mother! Daddy!"

It happened that the Mortons and the Clarks had gone for a walk into the woods. It had seemed safe to leave the children, for they had thought the river very shallow and did not know about the deep hole.

"That sounded like Honey Bunch's voice," declared Mrs. Morton. She stopped to listen. "I wonder if something is wrong."

"I thought I heard someone scream," said

Mr. Morton. "I'll go back to camp and see."

"Let's all go," suggested Mrs. Clark. "Somehow I feel very uneasy."

The grown-ups hurried back through the woods. They had no idea that Norman was in danger or they would have run every step of the way.

Honey Bunch was so excited she didn't know what to do. She ran along the slippery bank and tried to reach Norman, but he was too far out in the stream. She looked about for a long stick, but there wasn't a single one lying on the ground.

Norman was thrashing about wildly in the water. Honey Bunch knew he would drown if she didn't get him out.

"Help! Help!" she screamed.

The bushes parted and a man with a red beard stepped out into the sunlight. He was the hermit, but Honey Bunch didn't realize that until later.

The man saw Norman struggling in the water. He ran to the bank and waded right in. Then, just as he grasped the little fellow,

he too was swept from his feet into the hole.
Even though he went under water he kept
tight hold of the little boy.

Honey Bunch thought that both Norman
and the hermit would be drowned. She called
again for help, and this time she heard an
answering cry.

"Coming!" shouted Daddy Morton.

He and Mr. Clark ran from the woods.
They plunged into the water and dragged
both Norman and the hermit to safety.

"I don't think the little fellow swallowed
very much water," gasped the bearded man.

"I did too," sputtered Norman. "Gallons
and gallons."

Mr. Clark picked the boy up in his arms
and carried him toward the trailer. The
hermit started to move away.

"You can't leave before we've had a chance
to thank you," said Mr. Morton quickly. He
took the man by the arm. "Come along with
me. We'll all get a change of clothes and
something hot to drink."

Honey Bunch's father led the hermit to the

Robin. By this time Mrs. Clark and Mrs. Morton had reached the scene. They both told the stranger how grateful they were because he had saved Norman.

The little boy was put to bed and given hot broth. He liked the fuss which was made over him, but he was eager to get up and find out what the huge bird had hidden behind the falls.

"I'll not look until you're able to go with me, Norman," Honey Bunch promised her playmate kindly.

When she saw that he was all right she ran back to the *Robin.* The hermit had changed into one of Mr. Morton's suits. Honey Bunch had to look at him twice to be sure he was the same person. Why, he wasn't an old man at all. In nice clothes he seemed almost as young as her daddy.

Mrs. Morton was busy preparing soup. She allowed Honey Bunch to carry a cup of the steaming broth to the stranger.

"Thank you, little Miss," he said, smiling at her.

Honey Bunch sat opposite the hermit, trying not to stare at him. She had never seen such a long red beard before. There were so many questions she wished to ask him, too. Finally she couldn't keep still another moment.

"Why do folks call you a hermit?" she said.

"Honey Bunch!" Mrs. Morton spoke severely.

The stranger didn't appear displeased at the little girl's question. He smiled and replied:

"Well, perhaps it's because I live alone in the woods. You see, I have no family."

"And did you lose everything you had in the world?" inquired Honey Bunch gravely. She remembered what the man had once said to her and Norman.

"Yes, everything. My job, my standing in the community, my car—"

"Did you lose your hat too?" asked Honey Bunch. She had been leading up to this question.

"Why yes, I did lose a hat," replied the hermit in a strange voice. "A felt hat with initials in the band."

Honey Bunch jumped down from the couch. She ran to the closet and found the hat which had been hidden behind the falls.

"Is this yours?" she questioned, offering it to him.

"Yes, this *is* mine! I bought it when I lived in Plaza City. That was three years ago. Where did you find it?"

"Behind the waterfall. I think maybe a great big bird carried it there."

"Behind the waterfall," repeated the hermit, deeply puzzled. "How could a bird carry my hat there?"

Honey Bunch told him about watching the eagle from the stone hideout. She explained that Norman had fallen into the water because he had been so eager to learn what new thing the bird had hidden there.

"Perhaps that eagle picked up my hat at the scene of the wreck," said the hermit. "If only I could find that place again!"

"What wreck do you mean?" inquired Mr. Morton with interest.

"The story is a long one," sighed the hermit.

"I'll start at the beginning. My name is Lester Terry. Until three years ago I was a jewelry salesman, and lived in Plaza City."

"Misfortune overtook you?" asked Mrs. Morton kindly.

"Yes. One night I was driving in my car— it was very dark. As I rounded a sharp curve, the wheels skidded. The machine crashed through a wooden railing and fell over a steep cliff."

"How dreadful," murmured Mrs. Morton.

"I was knocked unconscious," went on Lester Terry. "When I woke up I was in a hospital. It was two weeks later before I could leave.

"My car had been completely wrecked. At the time of the accident I carried a small pouch of jewels with me. They belonged to a firm for which I worked. Upon leaving the hospital my first thought was to recover the missing valuables."

"Weren't they picked up at the time of the accident?" inquired Mr. Morton in surprise.

"Not so far as I could learn. The man who

brought me to the hospital was a tourist. After leaving me there he continued on his way. I tried time and again to find the scene of the accident, but I couldn't."

"You mean you couldn't remember where the accident occurred?" asked Mrs. Morton.

Lester Terry shook his head. "My mind seemed to be a blank. I had suffered a head injury. The jewelry firm accused me of having stolen the missing gems."

"That was very unjust," declared Mrs. Morton.

"Yes, I was all broken up over it. I used every penny of my savings to make up the loss." The hermit spoke bitterly. "As a reward, I was discharged. Since then I've lived as best I could away from people. For years I've searched but I've never been able to find that leather bag."

By this time Mr. and Mrs. Morton were quite certain that they knew what had become of Lester Terry's jewels. They had allowed the hermit to finish his story because they wished to make no mistake.

Honey Bunch's eyes were dancing with delight.   She sprang from the couch.

"I know what became of your jewelry!" she cried.   "We have it!"

Lester Terry smiled sadly.   He didn't take the little girl seriously at all.

"I think we really have your jewelry, Mr. Terry," said Mrs. Morton.   "I will show you the leather bag."

She brought it from a hiding place in the kitchenette.   Lester Terry's hand trembled as he fingered the bag.

"Yes, yes," he said eagerly, "this is mine. There were several fine bracelets, one set with large diamonds.   And a number of rings."

"I think you will find everything there," smiled Mrs. Morton.

"Tell me how you obtained this jewelry," requested the man.

"Honey Bunch found it behind the waterfall," said Mrs. Morton.

"The big bird must have carried it there just like he did your hat!" exclaimed the little girl.   "I'm sure it was the bird!"

Before anyone could say another word there came a loud rap on the door of the Morton trailer.

"Let me answer it," said Honey Bunch.

She thought that the visitor would be Norman. As it happened, the little boy was still in bed.

Opening the door, Honey Bunch drew in her breath sharply. A man stood there. He did not see the grown-ups in the trailer. He began to talk in a gruff voice.

"I've followed you all the way from Fairhaven," he said firmly. "I've come for my bag of jewels!"

Honey Bunch was terribly frightened. She couldn't move and she could hardly speak.

"I—I—" was all she could say.

The man was Jasper Crone!

"You give me the bag of jewels this minute!" the dreadful fellow demanded.

CHAPTER XV

A "FINDER" BIRD

BEFORE Honey Bunch had time to cry out, Daddy Morton came to the door.

"What brings you here, Mr. Crone?" he asked.

"I want my bag of jewels," said the man. "I know you have them here all right."

"And how do you know that?"

"Because a certain person told me," said the fellow crossly. "Your children were seen taking the bag of jewels from my car."

"Oh, from your car," repeated Daddy Morton. "Then you admit you were the person who broke into our trailer? You took the jewels from us."

Jasper Crone realized that he had said entirely too much. Daddy Morton had caught him very cleverly.

164

"What if I did take the jewels?" he blustered. "They belonged to me."

"Can you prove that?"

"Certainly I can," said the man. "Besides, no other person has claimed the bag."

"You're wrong there," replied Daddy Morton. "I think we have found the *real* owner of the jewels."

Mr. Terry came to the door to join the men.

"It will be very easy for me to prove my claim," he said quietly. "The firm for which I worked will identify the jewels as belonging to me."

"You have no case at all," Daddy Morton told Jasper Crone. "In fact, you will be lucky if we don't turn you over to the police."

The man lost all of his bluster then. He was afraid he might be arrested for trying to take the leather bag when it was not his own.

"I didn't really mean to steal," he muttered. "I just thought the jewels belonged as much to me as to anyone else. I'll not bother you any more."

The fellow turned and walked quickly away.

Honey Bunch and her parents never saw him again.

"There is no one to dispute your claim now," Daddy Morton told Lester Terry. "The jewels are yours."

"I can't believe my good fortune," the man murmured. "I had given up all hope of ever finding them. If it hadn't been for Honey Bunch I never would have recovered the jewels."

"Norman helped too," declared the little girl loyally.

She added that they never would have found the leather bag if it hadn't been for the huge bird.

"I should like to see this wonderful bird," declared Daddy Morton. "We'll watch for it to return."

"Maybe it will bring along some more treasure," Honey Bunch laughed.

She was very eager to learn what new object the bird might have hidden behind the waterfall, but the little girl had promised Norman she would not search for it unless he could go with her. Of course she hoped it would be soon.

By late afternoon Mrs. Clark said that Norman might get up and dress. He seemed to have suffered no ill effects from his ducking in the river.

"Now let's find out what that old eagle left hidden in the rocks!" cried the little boy.

Mrs. Clark quickly caught his hand and held him so that he could not squirm away.

"I'm afraid to have you go near that place again," she shivered. "You might fall into the water. I had no idea there was a deep hole close to our camp."

"I'll be careful," promised Norman.

Even then Mrs. Clark would not allow him to go. The little boy had to stand on the bank while Honey Bunch explored behind the waterfall.

"What do you see?" shouted Norman excitedly. "Did the big bird leave another bag of jewels?"

At first Honey Bunch couldn't see a thing. She groped about in the semi-darkness until her hand touched something soft and woolly. She backed up and brought the object into the light.

"Why, it's only a ragged sweater!" exclaimed Norman. He was very disappointed.

"There's nothing more behind the falls," Honey Bunch reported.

Mr. Terry took the sweater from the little girl's hand.

"This belongs to me too," he said. "It was in my car at the time of the accident."

"The bird must have found the wreckage," stated Mrs. Morton. "But I declare, I've never heard of such a strange thing before."

"Eagles have very strong talons," said Daddy Morton. "They have been known to carry away small animals."

At nightfall Mr. Terry returned to his cabin in the woods. He promised that he would visit the camp again in the morning.

He was as good as his word. But when Honey Bunch saw him come toward the *Robin*

she didn't recognize him for a minute. The
man had shaved off his long red beard, and
was very young looking.

"Why, you don't seem a bit like a hermit
now!" the little girl laughed as she ran to meet
him.

"No, you don't," said Norman.

"I don't feel like one either," smiled Mr.
Terry. "But I've been hiding behind my
whiskers long enough."

The salesman told Mr. and Mrs. Morton
that he planned to return to Plaza City. From
the sale of the jewels he would have enough
money to live comfortably.

"Oh, are you going to sell all the rings and
bracelets?" asked Honey Bunch, a little disappointed.

"No, not quite everything," replied the man
smilingly.

Then he reached inside his vest pocket and
took out a small gold ring with a bright green
stone.

"Let's see if it will fit," he said. "Give me
your hand, Honey Bunch."

He slipped the ring on the little girl's third finger. It was just the right size.

"Oh, is this for *me?*" she cried.

"Yes, I should like you to keep it," smiled the man. "It is little enough to give in return for finding my jewels."

Norman stood watching with a very long face. He wondered if Mr. Terry had forgotten that he had helped find the treasure too.

"And here is something for you, Norman," declared the salesman. "A different sort of ring."

The gift was a handsome silver napkin ring. Thanking Mr. Terry, the children ran to show their parents what they had received.

"I like my present best," said Norman, "because it is larger than yours, Honey Bunch."

"But my ring is prettier," declared the little girl proudly. "It has a bright green stone in it."

The Mortons and the Clarks planned to break camp the following day. They invited the salesman to ride with them as far as Plaza City.

Early in the morning the two trailers left the camp by the waterfall. Norman and Honey Bunch rode together in the Morton car. Every little while they kept glancing back toward the *Robin*. They whispered a great deal, too.

"You children seem to have an important secret," laughed Mrs. Morton.

Honey Bunch and Norman just giggled and would not say a word. They did have a secret indeed.

In a few minutes the *Robin* bounced over a hard bump in the road. At the same time there came a strange sound from inside the trailer. Everyone heard it.

"What was that?" cried Mrs. Morton, looking back.

Mr. Morton quickly put on the car brakes.

"That dreadful noise *is* coming from our trailer!" exclaimed Mrs. Morton. "You don't suppose a chicken—"

Her husband drew up alongside the road and the *Bluebird* stopped also. With the car engine turned off the noise was even louder.

"I don't see what it can be," said Daddy
Morton.

Just then he chanced to glance at the children. They both looked very guilty.

"What do you two know about the matter?"
he asked severely.

"Please, Daddy," said Honey Bunch in a
timid voice, "I think maybe he got out of the
sack."

"He? Who's he?"

"The eagle," explained Honey Bunch.
"Norman and I were taking him home to be
our finder bird."

"To be *what?*" asked Daddy Morton.

"Our finder bird," repeated Norman.
"That old eagle could hunt for treasure around
Barham. He's real smart at finding things."

Mrs. Morton leaned back weakly against the
car cushions.

"An eagle in our trailer!" she exclaimed.
"Oh, Norman, I suppose this was your idea."

"Why yes," said the little boy. "But Honey
Bunch helped me put him in the sack."

"It's a wonder you're both alive to tell the

tale," declared Mr. Morton. "An eagle is a dangerous bird."

"This one wasn't," boasted Norman. "When he came from behind the falls we caught him in a big sack and tied him up. But I guess he got out."

"It sounds that way," said Mr. Morton grimly. "I wonder what he's done to Lady Clare."

"Oh, we put her in the *Bluebird,*" said Honey Bunch.

The grown-ups hurried back to the *Robin.* When the door was opened they saw that the eagle was indeed out of the sack. A lamp had been broken and the cover pulled from the couch.

"I guess the bird doesn't like to ride in a trailer," said Honey Bunch.

"No bird or wild animal likes captivity," explained Mrs. Morton. "If we should try to take this eagle home it would die."

Daddy Morton opened the door wide. In a moment the great bird fluttered out and flew away.

"Norman, never do a thing like that again," scolded Mrs. Clark. "I guess you didn't understand about eagles."

The *Robin* was cleaned up and Lady Clare was put back into her own trailer home. Then the travelers started on their way again.

At Plaza City everyone said good-bye to Lester Terry. Then the two trailers went on toward Barham.

As the *Robin* pulled into the Morton driveway, Mrs. Miller came running out of doors. She lifted Honey Bunch from the car and gave her a great squeeze.

"Land sakes, it's good to have you folks back," she declared. "The house has been so empty and quiet."

Ida Camp came running across the lawn. She wanted to be the first one to say hello to Norman and Honey Bunch.

"Did you have a nice time?" asked the little girl.

"Oh, yes, just the nicest kind of a time," replied Honey Bunch. "See my new ring, Ida."

"It's real pretty," declared Ida. "Where did you get it, Honey Bunch?"

The little girl told her playmate all about the hermit and the strange finder bird. Ida thought it a shame that Norman had not been allowed to bring the eagle home with him.

"Mother says wild birds can't live in cities," explained Honey Bunch. "Besides, I don't think the eagle could have found any more treasure."

The trailer trip had been a wonderful success. Just the same, everyone was glad to be in Barham again. Lady Clare was especially pleased at being home once more. She had missed her bed by the stove.

"I worried a lot about that cat," said Mrs. Miller. "I thought she had run away."

"Didn't you get my letter?" asked Mother.

"Yes," replied the laundress. "After that I didn't worry. I guess Lady Clare made up her mind she needed a trailer vacation too."

"Now that the trip is over, there is only one thing that bothers me," remarked Mr. Morton.

"What is that, Daddy?"

"I wish I could sell the trailer."

"Oh, can't we use it next year too?" asked Honey Bunch.

Daddy Morton said if they should decide upon a second trailer vacation it would be easy to buy another "rolling house." The *Robin* would take up too much space in the meantime.

Mr. Clark had the *Bluebird* hauled back to the rental shop, but for several days the *Robin* stood in the Mortons' back yard.

Honey Bunch and Norman were very proud of the *Robin*. They showed it to all their little friends, but they could see that the trailer was killing all the nice lawn grass beneath it. It was very much in the way when they played tag, too.

One afternoon the Mortons were surprised to see Mr. and Mrs. Victor Dare drive into town. The couple spent several hours at the Morton home and heard all about Lester Terry. They laughed heartily when they heard of Norman's finder bird.

"I am glad Jasper Crone will cause no more

trouble," declared Mrs. Dare. "I'll always believe he was the one who set fire to our trailer."

Mrs. Morton asked if the Dares had made any plans for the future.

"Oh, we'll start another puppet show," replied Mr. Dare. "We have everything bought for it now. That is, everything except a trailer."

He then went on to say that he would like to buy the *Robin*. Mr. Morton was very pleased to sell. The men made a deal, and the next morning the Dares came to drive the big red trailer away.

"How about taking Honey Bunch too?" joked Mrs. Dare. She smiled at the little girl. "Wouldn't you like to go along with us? You could help us run the puppet show."

"Well, yes," said Honey Bunch politely. She knew the woman didn't really mean to take her away. "But I think maybe Mother and Daddy would miss me."

"We couldn't spare our little girl," laughed Mrs. Morton.

Mr. and Mrs. Dare shook hands with their friends.

"I hope we'll see you again next summer," said the puppet show lady, climbing into the car. "Have you made your plans?"

"Not yet," replied Mrs. Morton. "But we always try to go to some interesting place."

And the Mortons always did. Very soon they were to take their little girl and her cousin Stub on a wonderful vacation. It will be called, "Honey Bunch: Her First Trip to a Big Fair."

Honey Bunch glanced up and smiled. It would be fun seeing new places next year. But she couldn't imagine any nicer vacation than the one she had just had—her first trip in a trailer.

THE END